THROUGH EUROPE WITH NAPOLEON

This edition published 2025
by Living Book Press
Copyright © Living Book Press, 2025

ISBN: 978-1-76153-375-4 (hardcover)
          978-1-76153-376-1 (softcover)

First published in 1908.

Through Europe
With Napoleon

by

HENRIETTA E. MARSHALL

Contents

Napoleon as a boy

CHAPTER I

ABOUT A ROCKY ISLAND IN THE BLUE SEA

To the south of Europe there lies a blue sea called the Mediterranean. Its name means "in the middle of the land," and if you look on the map you will see that land shuts it in on every side, its only outlet to the ocean being by the Straits of Gibraltar. For this reason the ancients called it "the sea in the middle of the land," "the inner sea," or "our sea," and to them it was the centre of trade of the world, for the lands of nearly all the world they knew lay about it.

The Mediterranean is very blue. This is partly because it lies in the south, and the sunny blue skies above it are reflected in its waters; partly because it is so deep. In places it is forty or fifty times deeper than our grey North Sea. It is far more salt, too. There are two reasons for this. First, because not many large rivers empty themselves into the Mediterranean; and second, because the warm sun of the south draws up a great deal of the water, leaving the salt behind.

In this sunny, blue sea lies the island of Corsica. It is a rugged and beautiful little island, full of high mountains. Except a strip of land on the eastern shore, looking towards Italy, there is hardly any plain in it. What plain there is, is very fertile, and much of the island is thickly wooded. Here are orange and lemon groves; here mulberries, olives, and beautiful grapes grow and ripen; and the trade of the island consists largely in the export of fruit and timber.

Corsica lies about fifty miles from the coast of Italy, and for hundreds of years the island belonged to the Republic of Genoa. The people are hardy and brave, and, like all mountain peoples, they love liberty. They hated to be ruled by Genoa, and at last, under a leader called Paoli, they rebelled and fought for freedom. So well did they fight that they nearly drove the Genoese out. Then the Genoese asked the French to help them, and at last, tired of the struggle, they sold the island to France.

At that the Corsicans were very angry. "What right had the Genoese to sell them like cattle to a new master?" they asked. So they went on fighting the French, as they had fought the Genoese.

Among those who fought were Charles – Marie Bonaparte and his brave wife, Letizia. Bonaparte was an Italian, but for many years his family had lived in Corsica. He was a noble; but in Corsica there was little difference between nobles and shep-herds—they were all poor and proud alike. Letizia was young and beautiful, yet she bore all the hardships of war bravely. She followed her husband even to the battle-field. She was often in danger from flying bullets, yet she feared nothing, and thought only of the safety of her husband and the freedom of her country. By mountain paths, steep and narrow; through trackless forests, called in Corsica, "maquis"; over streams where there were no bridges, Letizia followed her husband. She was only a girl, but she had the heart of a hero, and not until the struggle proved hopeless did she give in.

For France was great and Corsica little, and brave though the people were, they were at last forced to yield and become part of the French dominion; and their leader Paoli fled over the seas.

So there was peace. But it was the peace between slave and tyrant. The Corsicans hated the French, and many of the French were not greatly pleased with their new possession. It was but a useless mass of rock, they said. It would never be anything but a burden. It cost so much to keep the people in subjection that one

Frenchman said he wished he could bore a hole in the bottom of the island and sink it in the sea, and so have done with it.

And here, in this little island, almost before the roar of battle had ceased, among a people full of sullen anger and bitterness against their conquerors, a little son was born, one blazing August day in 1769, to Charles and Letizia Bonaparte. They gave him the name of Napoleon, but he was not baptized until he was nearly two years old. Then, on the same day that his sister Anna Maria was baptized in the Cathedral of Ajaccio, the capital of Corsica, he received the name which he was to make famous all the world over, and for all time to come.

The house in which Napoleon was born is still shown in Ajaccio. Long ago, however, it was plundered and burned down, and although it has been built again, we cannot say if is really like the house in which he was born or not. But the square in which it stands is still called Letizia Place, and all about the little town of Ajaccio are things which remind one of the small dark-faced boy, who grew up to be one of the greatest men who has ever lived.

CHAPTER II

LESSONS AND PLAY

Napoleon had several brothers and sisters, and their mother, having only one servant, had a great deal to do, and not much time to look after the children. So she gave them a big, empty room in which to play. The walls and floor of this room were bare, and there was nothing in it except the children's toys. Here they were allowed to do as they liked. They scribbled and drew pictures on the walls, and played at all sorts of games. Napoleon always drew soldiers marching to battle, and played with nothing but a drum and a wooden sword. He used to get up battles, too, between the boys of Ajaccio and the boys of the neighbourhood. These wars would last for months at a time, during which there would be many pitched battles, surprises, and assaults. Napoleon, of course, was always leader, and made the others obey him. He was afraid of no one, and he bit, scratched, and slapped any one, big or little, as he chose. He was often noisy and quarrelsome, and bullied his brothers and sisters, especially Joseph, who was older than he.

But at times, too, even when he was a very small boy, he would be moody and thoughtful, and would walk about by himself, refusing to speak or play with the others. He was an untidy little boy, not caring in the least how he was dressed. His straight dark hair straggled over his brown face, and his stockings hung down over his shoe-tops, and altogether he must have looked a wild little harum-scarum.

When Napoleon was about five years old he was sent to a school for little girls kept by nuns. Here he learned to read and to do sums. He became so fond of sums, and so good at them, that the nuns called him the little mathematician.

Soon Napoleon left the nuns' school and went to a boys' school, along with his brother Joseph. Here the boys in class were set opposite each other in two rows, each under a large flag. One was the flag of Carthage, the other the flag of Rome, with S.P.Q.R. upon it, which means "Senatus Populusque Romanus." That is Latin for "The Senate and People of Rome."

The boys were arranged like this so that each side might try to learn better than the other, and fight and conquer in lessons, as the Romans and Carthaginians fought in war.

As Napoleon was the younger of the two brothers, he was put on the side of Carthage. But he did not like that at all, for in history he knew the Romans had always been the conquerors, and he liked to be on the winning side. So Joseph, who did not mind so much, changed with Napoleon, and allowed him to be a Roman.

Napoleon worked hard at his lessons. By the time he was eight he was so fond of arithmetic that his mother had a little room built for him in the garden, where he might work without being bothered by his brothers and sisters. There he used to spend many hours making all kinds of calculations. But even more than sums he loved soldiers. Every morning, before he went to school, he was given a piece of white bread. This he used to give to a soldier in exchange for a piece of coarse brown soldiers' bread. His mother was not very pleased at this. "Why do you give away your good white bread for a piece of brown?" she asked him one day.

"Because," replied Napoleon, "if I am going to be a soldier I must get used to eating soldiers' bread. Besides, I like it."

As Napoleon loved soldiers so much, his father and mother decided that he should be one. And one December day a little ship sailed away from Corsica, carrying Charles Bonaparte and his two sons, Joseph and Napoleon, over the sea to France. Napoleon was not yet ten, and Joseph scarcely a year more. He was going to learn to be a priest, and Napoleon to be a soldier.

Corsica lies about a hundred miles from the shores of France,

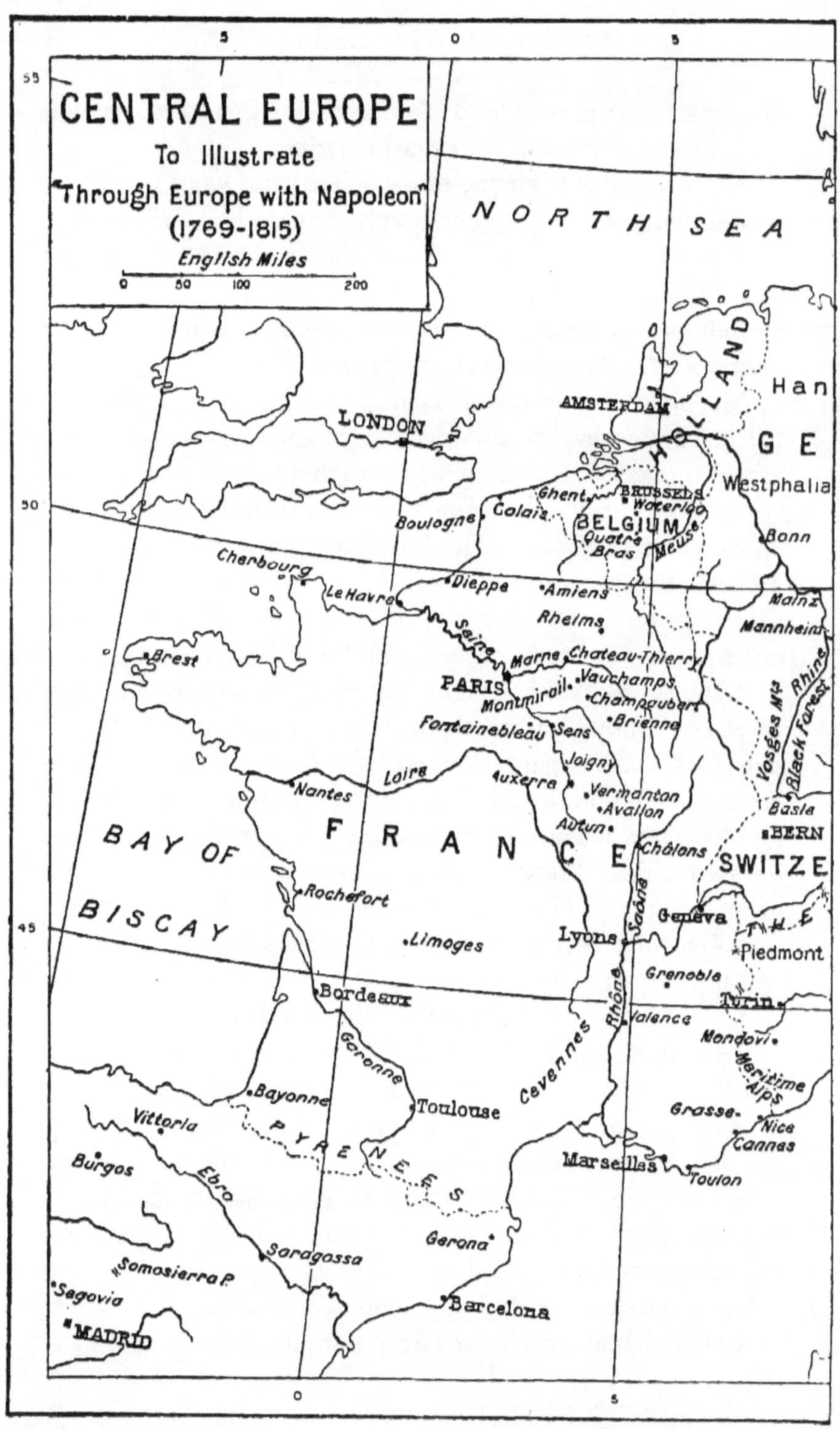

CENTRAL EUROPE
To Illustrate
"Through Europe with Napoleon"
(1769-1815)
English Miles
0   50   100   200
NORTH SEA
LONDON
AMSTERDAM
HOLLAND
Han
GE
Westphalia
Ghent
BRUSSELS
Waterloo
BELGIUM
Quatre Bras
Meus
Bonn
Boulogne
Calais
Mainz
Mannheim
Cherbourg
Le Havre
Dieppe
Amiens
Rheims
Seine
Marne
Chateau-Thierry
Brest
Vauchamps
PARIS
Montmirail
Champaubert
Brienne
Fontainebleau
Sens
Vosges Mts
Rhine
Black Forest
Joigny
Auxerre
Vermanton
Avallon
Basle
Autun
BERN
Nantes
Loire
Châlons
SWITZE
F R A N C E
Saône
BAY OF
Geneva
TYROL
Piedmont
Rochefort
Limoges
Lyons
Grenoble
B I S C A Y
Rhône
Turin
Bordeaux
Valence
Mondovi
Garonne
Cevennes
Maritime Alps
Bayonne
Toulouse
Grasse
Vittoria
P Y R E N E E S
Nice
Cannes
Burgos
Ebro
Marseilles
Toulon
Gerona
Saragossa
Somosierra P.
Segovia
Barcelona
MADRID

10 15 20 25
55
DENMARK
COPENHAGEN
Memel
Tilsit
Niemen
Konigsberg
Preuss. Friedland
Eylau
Alle
Pregel
Danzig
Hamburg
Bremen
Elbe
over
Kustrin
Posen
Warsaw
Spandau
Vistula
BERLIN
Dennewitz
Oder
Warthe
Poland
Magdeburg
RMAN EMPIRE
Leipzig
Bunst-
lau
Liegnitz
Naumburg
Grosz
Dresden
Breslau
Auerstadt
Goschen
Pirna
Bautzen
Silesia
Erfurt
Jena
Zittau
Saxony
Saalfield
Erz Geb
Kulm
50
Frankfurt
Prague
Galicia
Hanau
Neckar
Bohemia
Bavaria
Brünn
Austerlitz
Regensburg
Wurtemburg
Isar
Danube
Wagram
Aspern Essling
Ulm
Augsburg
Pressburg
VIENNA
Munich
AUSTRIA-HUNGARY
RLAND
Tyrol
A L P S
Danube
45
Venetia
Trieste
Lombardy
Verona
Fiume
Milan
Lodi
Venice
Po
Mantua
Marengo
Modena
Bosnia
SERVIA
Parma
Bologna
Genoa
A
20
P
Leghorn
Pistoia
E
Florence
N
N
Elba
ITALY
I
Corsica
N
Ajaccio
ROME
E
S
Sardinia
Naples
10 15
BATTLEFIELDS OF BELGIUM
Oudenarde
Grammont
BRUSSELS
Enghien
Halle
Waterloo
Liege
Brain le Comte
Quatre Bras
Seraing
Nivelles
Ligny
Namur
Charleroi
Philippeville
Givet
ADRIATIC SEA
Bartholomew Edin.

but from Ajaccio to Marseilles, to which Bonaparte now sailed, is two hundred miles or more.

Marseilles is a very ancient town. It was founded by the Greeks hundreds of years ago. They called it Marsalia. The people of Marsalia became great sailors and traders, and were masters of the Mediterranean. Now Marseilles is the chief sea-port of France and the second city of the Republic, Paris only being bigger.

Marseilles does not lie, like so many of our great ports, on the estuary of a river—it is a deep-sea port, not a river port. A deep-sea port has an advantage over a river port in that larger vessels can come into harbour, as a rule. But, on the other hand, without a river behind the port it is neither so easy nor so cheap to carry goods inland. So people have talked of making a canal to join Marseilles with the Rhône, which flows into the Mediterranean not far off. The Rhône, however, although it is the largest river of France, is not very good for navigation. It rises high among the Swiss mountains, and therefore flows very swiftly. It is so shallow, too, that going up-stream steamers have to go empty, or only half laden. So that trade by way of the Rhône is more export than import. But its tributary the Saone, which joins it at Lyons, flows slowly, and is of much use for trade. By canals it is connected with other French rivers and with the Rhine, the great German river, and so the valley of the Rhône has become the natural trade route from the south.

Much of the trade of the Mediterranean passes through Marseilles, but it has two rivals in Trieste and Genoa. In Britain, of two ports the one may rise and the other fall, for some reason or another, but still the wealth brought by trade remains in the country, although it may have gone to another town. On the Continent, however, two rival ports near each other may be in different lands. Then the rivalry between them grows keener.

Marseilles lies in the warm and fertile Rhône valley, where olive and mulberry trees grow, so it does great trade in oil and silk. It imports raw silk too from the East, which it sends to the silk-mills of Lyons. Thousands of sheep are imported every year from Algiers, so in Marseilles large factories of soap and candles, boots and shoes have arisen.

CHAPTER III

SCHOOL DAYS

Up the fertile valley of the Rhône, beneath the shadow of the Cevennes, beside the rushing river, past the city of Lyons, with its famous silk factories, then by the slow-flowing Saône Napoleon passed, until, a fortnight after he and his father and brother had set out, they arrived at the town of Autun.

Here, in this busy manufacturing town, with its fine cathedral and grey remains of Roman times, the boys were sent to school. With his fellows Joseph soon became a favourite. He was a little shy at first, but he was lively and gay, and joined in games with the other boys.

Napoleon, on the other hand, was silent and sad. His dark face looked sulky, and instead of joining in the games, he liked best to go about by himself. So the boys teased him. They called him "cowardly Corsican," and reminded him that his island had been conquered by the French. At first Napoleon paid no attention. Then suddenly, one day, flashing round on his tormentors, he cried, "If the French had been four against one only, they would never have had Corsica: but they were ten to one."

But if Joseph was a greater favourite, Napoleon was far more clever. He soon learned to read and speak in French. For to the boys French was a foreign language; at home, in Corsica, they spoke Italian. And although Napoleon learned to speak French very well, all his life long he made mistakes in it, especially in writing. He wrote very badly too—to hide his bad spelling, some people say.

The little, sulky, lonely boy did not stay long at Autun. In about three months his father came to take him away to the military school at Brienne. But Joseph was to be left at Autun. The two brothers had never before been parted, and although Napoleon bullied Joseph they were very fond of each other. Now that they were in a strange land, far from their home, among people speaking a strange language, they seemed to love each other more. When they knew that they must part, Joseph burst into tears. But Napoleon tried hard to pretend that he did not care. His dark face only looked more sulky than before. But although he tried hard, he could not quite keep back the tears, and one slowly trickled down his cheek.

Brienne is more than a hundred miles north of Autun, and was in those days a long journey, when there were no trains, and travellers had to ride or drive all the way. Brienne lies near the Aube, a tributary of the Seine, in that part of France called Champagne, from which the wine champagne takes its name. But Brienne itself is now chiefly famous as the place where Napoleon was at school. Before the town hall there stands a statue of him as he looked when a boy.

The school to which Napoleon was now sent was one of twelve founded by King Louis XVI. for the children of nobles too poor to give their sons a good education. Once a boy was received as a king's scholar, he was obliged to remain at school for six years, and was not allowed to go home, even for holidays, without special leave.

Although these schools were called military schools, they were taught by monks, and were really not very different from other schools. The boys, however, wore a uniform, and Napoleon was now dressed in a suit of blue with red facings and white metal buttons.

At first Napoleon was not happy at this school, even though he was dressed in a uniform and was going to be a soldier. He was dreadfully homesick. The dull, chalky downs of Champagne seemed to him dismal and uninteresting after beautiful Corsica, with its hills and glens and sunny blue sky. And here, in this dull land, he must remain for six years! To a little boy of nine it seemed as if six years would never end.

As Napoleon was shy, moody, and silent, his schoolfellows teased him. They nicknamed him "Straw on Nose," because they thought that he held his nose in the air, and that Napoleon sounded like the French words for straw on nose—"la paille au nez." They teased him, too, about his country. "You are a conquered nation, a people of slaves," they said.

This always made Napoleon fierce. "I hope one day to give my country freedom," he would cry.

Even the masters made him angry, because they taught that Corsica was Italian, and Napoleon hated the Italians almost as much as he hated the French. So he sulked, and grew angry, and ended by hating all his schoolfellows. "I will do these Frenchmen as much harm as I can," he said. They, in their turn, disliked him, although many of them feared him, and allowed themselves to be ordered about by him.

Each boy had a piece of ground given to him for a garden. Napoleon made two of the others give their gardens to him. Round them and his own, he made a fence and planted bushes which in two years grew so thick that no one could see through. Here Napoleon used to spend all his playtime alone, reading and thinking. And woe to any one who dared to come near to disturb him!

CHAPTER IV

MORE SCHOOL DAYS

After Napoleon had been at school for some time, the boys were all formed into an army. They were drilled, had to obey orders, and form and march in line, like real soldiers. And as in a real army, some were officers. Napoleon was given the rank of captain. But his schoolfellows made up their minds to show him how they hated him. They held a council of war, and declared that Napoleon was unworthy to hold any rank, because he had shown that he did not care in the least for any of them. This sentence was read to him, and then they took away his gold braid and signs of office, and degraded him to the ranks.

But instead of flying into a fierce passion, as they had expected, Napoleon took his humiliation so quietly that the boys, in place of feeling pleased with what they had done, were sorry. They were not really cruel, and were quite willing to be friends. And Napoleon, surprised that they should try to be kind, came out of his shell and became more sociable.

Instead of being the butt of the whole school, he now for a time became a sort of captain of games. He had read about the Olympic games and the Roman circus, so now he arranged wrestling and races, in imitation of them. He got up battles, too, one side being Greeks or Romans, the other side Persians or Carthaginians. But this brought Napoleon into trouble, for the warriors used stones for ammunition, and some of the boys were hurt. So the headmaster put an end to such dangerous games, and scolded Napoleon severely as he was the ringleader. This made the proud Corsican boy angry, and once more he took to sulking alone.

One winter, when Napoleon had been about four years at school, the boys had lessons about the building of ramparts and fortifications. They were taught the names of the different kinds of forts, their uses, and how best to attack and defend them. While these lessons were going on, there came a heavy fall of snow. This gave Napoleon a grand idea. Instead of fighting like the ancient Greeks and Romans, they would build a fortress of snow, and attack and defend it like modern soldiers.

All the boys were delighted with the idea. Napoleon drew out the lines of the fort, and soon every one was hard at work with spade and wheelbarrow, eagerly building under Napoleon's directions.

When the fort was finished, the boys took sides, and fought with snowballs. Napoleon was general, and he commanded both sides, giving orders sometimes to the besiegers, sometimes to the defenders. This time the masters were quite pleased, and looked on, cheering those boys who showed most courage and cleverness.

Soon the fame of the fort spread far, and people came from all round about to see it and watch the fights. These went on as long as the snow lay upon the ground. But at last March came, the sun began to grow warm, the snow melted, and the storming and snowballing came to an end. The masters were not sorry when this happened, as many of the boys had caught bad colds from playing so much in the snow. As for Napoleon, he was more sure than ever that the life of a soldier was the grandest possible, and he felt that he was born to make others obey him.

As to his lessons, Napoleon learned no Greek, and never did his Latin well. He loved the tales of the Greek and Roman heroes, but he read them in translations. It seemed to him waste of time to try to read them in a dead or foreign language. At arithmetic and geometry he was good. He liked his geography lessons too, but above all he loved history. Whenever he had a spare moment he might be found reading, and it was history and the lives of great men that he read. Indeed he often read when he ought to have been playing games. So he never grew tall; and although his shoulders were broad, he was thin and delicate-looking.

Only once, during all the years that Napoleon was at Brienne, did he see his father. It was in the little bare parlour of the school where visitors were received that father and son met after five long years. Charles Bonaparte had left a child, he found a man, for although Napoleon was only fifteen he spoke and thought as a man. We can imagine what joy it was to him to have news of his dearly-loved home from one who had seen it lately, and how sad he was when his father went away again.

Napoleon never saw his father again, for handsome Charles Bonaparte was already very ill, and a few months afterwards he died. He never knew what a great man his son was to be. Yet it is said that when he lay a-dying he called aloud for him. "Where is my son Napoleon? Where is my son, whose sword will make kings tremble, who will change the face of the earth?"

CHAPTER V

FROM BRIENNE TO PARIS

Now came the question of what Napoleon was to be, whether soldier or sailor. He himself wanted to go into the navy. But his mother, who loved him dearly, could not bear the thought of so much danger—danger from shot and shell, and from the angry waves too. So Napoleon gave up that idea, and resolved to go into the artillery.

He had still another year, he thought, to pass in Brienne, when one day he was told that he had been admitted to the military school at Paris. And on the 30th of October 1784 he set out for the capital with four other boys.

We can hardly think that Napoleon was sorry to leave Brienne. Yet long years after, when his life of blood and fame was over, and he was a prisoner in a lonely island, his thoughts turned to that rugged country, "the fatherland of his thought," he called it.

It was in dull November weather that this passionate and moody Corsican boy first saw beautiful Paris, "the City of Light." Paris is not only the capital—it is the very heart of France; and at the call of Paris every town and village answers and thrills. All the history of France is wrapped in Paris. Which way it leads, to wild revolution, to empire, to democracy, France follows.

It is here that the ruler, be he King, Emperor, or President, lives. Here meets the Parliament, and here the laws for the ruling of the land are made. Paris is not only the largest town in France—it is the largest on the Continent. It is a city of beauty and splendour, made, it would seem, for sunshine, light, and happiness. Full of broad streets and stately palaces, crowned with pinnacles and domes, it lies amid its hills, a very queen of cities. Yet this gay city, clothed with such airy grace, breathing of mirth and laughter, has seen days of horror and darkness. The howl of maddened multitudes, the roar of starving, frenzied mobs, has sounded through its stately halls. The fair streets have been sodden with trampled blood, the glorious palaces, wrecked with fire and sword, have been laid in ruins, and the fair face of Paris has been scarred and seared. Yet the finger of time has smoothed away every trace of agony and passion, and still Paris, ever young, though so full of memories, smiles upon the world.

But although Paris has beauty and power, and is full of history and romance, it has much else too. It lies upon the Seine, the best navigable river of France, just where the Marne, another good navigable stream, joins it. And up and down the river, day and night, go ships laden with merchandise. From Paris as a centre, railroads lead out to every port of France, for it is the heart of all the foreign trade.

Paris, too, in spite of its brightness and beauty, is a city of work and factories. Here are manufactures of machinery, carriages, motors; here are tanneries and boot factories; factories of furniture and perfumes, of china, clocks, and pianos, and an endless list of things. But especially it is famous for its jewellery and its beautiful little trifles, called "articles de Paris." These find a market among the wealthy people of Paris itself, and are easily sent to the still greater and wealthier city of London.

And besides all this, Paris has a University, and is famous for its schools of painting and sculpture.

And now the man who was to play upon this Paris, and to play upon France, and make them answer to his will, was quietly learning his lessons in the school upon the Champs de Mars—the Field of the War-God.

At Paris, as at Brienne, Napoleon worked hard. But although sometimes he still shut himself up in moody silence, he mixed far more with his fellow-students, and took part in their games. The truth was, he was now in his element. It seemed to Napoleon that he was no longer at school, but in a city under arms and in a state of war. His masters were no longer monks, but soldiers. All around him he saw men in uniforms. He was no longer awakened from sleep or called to class by the sound of a bell, but by the rat-tat of a drum. Sentinels marched to and fro. Every hour, by night or day, he heard the sharp word of command, the ring and thud of grounding muskets. All the talk was of war, and the boys discussed together the regiments to which they would belong, their uniforms, and arms. So, among sights and sounds that he loved, Napoleon opened out and became more friendly.

Yet still above all things he remained a Corsican, loving his native land with a fierce love. He began to write a poem on the liberty of Corsica, and recited it to one of his fellows with great gusto, waving a rusty old sword in his hand. Sometimes he would march up and down the fencing-school his hands behind him, his chin thrust forward, dreaming of how one day he would free his dear land. If his schoolfellows laughed at him and called him "Corsican," he would seize a fencing-stick and cry, "Come on, I'll fight you all," and so in shouts of scorn and laughter would end his dream.

One of his schoolfellows drew a caricature of Napoleon on the blank page in his atlas, marching to help Paoli, while an old professor is trying to hold him back by the pigtail. Underneath he wrote, "Napoleon, run, fly to help Paoli, and deliver him out of the hands of his enemies." So in many ways he was teased and laughed at.

At length the heads of the school heard about it. It seemed to them that in his love for his island Napoleon was forgetting his duty to the King, so he was ordered to appear before them. "You are a King's scholar," they said; "you must remember that, and moderate your love for Corsica, which, after all, is part of France."

But Napoleon could not moderate his love, and when he remembered that the French had conquered Corsica he hated them.

CHAPTER VI

NAPOLEON BECOMES LIEUTENANT

When Napoleon had been a year in Paris he passed his examinations, and received his commission as second lieutenant in the artillery regiment of La Fère, one of the finest in the army.

Although Napoleon had been a year in Paris he knew nothing of the beautiful city. He had hardly ever been beyond the gates of the school, in the Champs de Mars. Now he spent two days paying visits and wandering about the great town. But even yet he was considered as a schoolboy. Everywhere a non-commissioned officer went with him.

On the 30th of October 1785 Napoleon and another boy, called Des Mazis, with whom he had grown very friendly, set out to join their regiment at Valence. They were only boys of sixteen and seventeen, but they felt very grand, for now they were real officers. They wore swords and belts and silver collar-clasps. But to their great grief they were not yet allowed to wear the uniform of their regiment, but had to travel in their school uniforms. Still, it was a fine thing to wear a sword. So they climbed joyfully into the Lyons coach, and were soon whirling away southwards behind spanking horses.

Soon after they started they passed through the forest of Fontainebleau, one of the finest in France. It is famous for its beautiful walks through rugged gorges, for the ground is very rocky, and there are many quarries, both of building and paving stones, in the forest. The streets of Paris are paved, for the most part, with stones from Fontainebleau. Here, too, is a splendid palace, once a favourite country-house of the Kings of France. Little did one of the boys think that the day would come when he would live in that beautiful palace, and that he should pass there some of the bitterest moments of his life.

At Fontainebleau the boys dined, and that evening they reached the little town of Sens, in the department of Yonne. Yonne is one of the most hilly parts of the basin of the Seine, and its rocky slopes are clad with vines, from which very good wine is made.

Next day, following the valley of the Yonne, they went on by Joigny, Auxerre, Avallon, and Vermanton, all famous for their wine trade.

Next they passed by Saulieu, just crossing into the department of Côte-d'Or, fertile and famous for its wheat fields and pasture lands. Then on again to Autun, where Napoleon had been once before and stayed a few months at school, arriving at last at Chalons-sur-Saône, in the agricultural department of Saône-et-Loire.

Saône-et-Loire is one of the most fertile departments of France, and Chalons has been called the "granary of wheat." Besides wheat, excellent wines are produced, and indeed it is so fertile, and the climate is so good, that, except olive trees, nearly everything grows here which is found in the warmest and sunniest parts of France.

At Chalons the boys left the coach, and took boat upon the slow-flowing Saóne. As far as Lyons they had a pleasant journey, for the river was as smooth as a canal. Lyons is the third city of France. Lying in the warm and fertile valley of the Rhône, where great quantities of mulberry trees, upon which silkworms feed, grow, it is the chief centre of silk manufacture, and half of the silk of the whole world passes through its markets. The water is good for dyeing silk, there are coal and iron mines not far off, so it is not wonderful that Lyons has become a great manufacturing town.

At Lyons the boys left the Saône, and began their journey down the Rhône. Even they could not help seeing the difference in the rivers. Now, instead of flowing smoothly through a pleasant valley, the stream rushed along through wild and rugged country.

The very sailors seemed to change with the scenery, and become rough and wild like their land.

At last the long journey ended at Valence. Valence is a very old town. The Romans called it Valentia. It is a manufacturing town, where silk, gloves, glass, paper, and many other things are made.

The La Fère regiment, being one of the best, was one of the most hard-working of the French artillery. The men got up early, and worked hard at marching, drilling, and shooting. Napoleon was in a way still a pupil. He had to begin at the bottom, and serve first as a gunner, then as corporal and sergeant, so that he might know his work in every detail. Then only was he considered fit to be an officer.

One of Napoleon's first duties as an officer was helping to put down a riot among the silk-workers of Lyons. At this time in the history of France these riots and strikes had become very common. The King, Louis XVI., kept a splendid court, and spent a great deal of money. To get this money the people were year by year taxed more and more heavily, and became poorer and poorer, until some of them lived in the most utter misery and wretchedness, having scarcely enough to eat. Then they rebelled. Soon the rebellion spread all over France, and what is called the French Revolution began.

CHAPTER VII

NAPOLEON VISITS HIS OLD HOME

After Napoleon came back from Lyons, he went home to Corsica, on leave. It was the first time that he had seen his native land, his mother, brothers, and sisters, for nearly eight years. To find himself once more in his dear island, among the woods and gardens where he had played as a child, was great joy. He was never tired of wandering through the valleys, of climbing the hills, of making friends with the shepherds in their lonely huts, sometimes spending whole days and nights with them.

At this time Madame Bonaparte was very poor. She had still four little children to bring up and send to school. She was so poor that she could keep no servant. Napoleon's pay as a lieutenant was only about £50 a year. Out of that he had to pay for food and lodgings and buy his uniform. But he managed to help his mother too, and pay some of his brothers' schooling.

The rules about leave do not seem to have been very strict, for, in one way or another, Napoleon had leave from his regiment for a year and nine months. Part of this time he spent in Paris. Then for the first time he began to know something about the beautiful town, and often spent hours wandering alone through the streets.

But at last, in June 1788, he was obliged to go back to his regiment. While Napoleon had been away it had been moved from Valence to Auxonne, a little commercial and manufacturing town upon the Saône.

The country round Auxonne was marshy and damp, for the

Saône often overflowed its banks, and for some months in the winter Napoleon became quite ill. But when spring came, and the damp fogs went, he grew better.

Here, as at Valence, Napoleon worked hard. Besides drilling and practising gunnery, he read everything he could about soldiers. He learned to draw maps and plans, and as he was one of the keenest, soon became one of the cleverest, of the officers of the regiment.

But he did not spend all his time in work. He had his share too in all the fun and jokes of which his companions were fond. He took part in dinners, balls, and parties. Indeed since he had become an officer, Napoleon was no longer the moody boy he had been, although at times he might have fits of passion.

But meanwhile, as the days and months went on, great changes were taking place in France.

At this time the position of King and people in France was very different from what it was in Britain. The people of Britain, through long years of struggle, had gained freedom. Their King was a limited monarch; that is, the power of the King was held in check by Lords and Commons. But in France there was no check upon the King. He could do as he liked. Under him there were the "three estates", that is, the nobles, the clergy, and the people. The nobles and the clergy paid no taxes. They were called the privileged classes. They and the King spent a great deal of money. So the third estate—that is, the people—had to pay. Every year the King and nobles spent more and more. Every year the people had to pay more and more.

As the years went on the people grew more and more miserable, and more and more weary of their rulers. Many of them were very ignorant. They hardly knew what was wrong, or how it might be put right. They only knew that they were poor, miserable, and hungry. Riots, such as you have already heard about, grew more and more frequent; all the summer of 1789 was stormy with them. At last the people broke out fiercely in Paris. They seized and pulled down the state prison. The King and his advisers were powerless. "It is revolt," said he, when he heard of it.

"Nay, sire," replied his minister, "it is revolution."

The revolt spread fast. In July there was a riot in Auxonne. The crowd seized the tax-collector, burst into the custom-houses, wrecked them, and smashed the furniture. The soldiers were called out, but they did little more than look on. They surrounded the rioters, but did not try to stop them. The soldiers themselves were of the people, and they felt with them.

A few weeks later many of the soldiers mutinied and joined the rioters. Soon all over France the revolution was blazing. Everything was turned topsy-turvy, and men knew not whom to follow.

But Napoleon was no Frenchman. He was a Corsican. The troubles of France did not touch him, except that he thought perhaps good might come to his dear island out of them. And so in this time of wild unrest he asked for leave and went home once more.

For the next four years Napoleon divided his time between France and Corsica. Indeed he spent so much of his time in Corsica that at one time his commission was taken away from him. But he gave such good excuses for having been absent that the Minister of War allowed him to go back to his post with the rank of captain.

Napoleon saw France pass through some of the worst days of blood and terror, but he took no part in them. At this time the lesser struggles of his own island seemed to him more important.

Corsica, like France, was in a state of turmoil and anarchy. Paoli, the great Corsican hero, had returned from exile, and was everywhere greeted with cheers.

At first Napoleon loved and honoured his hero, as he had when a boy. But soon these two, the grey old hero whose work was done, and the brown-faced lad whose work was only beginning, quarrelled. The story of these quarrels is hard to follow, but at last Napoleon, who had been so great a patriot, took the side of France. Then he and all his family were forced to flee from Corsica in secret, and after many adventures they arrived safely in Marseilles. There Napoleon left his mother and sisters in great poverty, and went to join his regiment, which was now at Nice. From henceforth he was a French-man.

CHAPTER VIII

TOULON

When the French rebelled against their King, many of the princes and rulers of the other countries of Europe joined together and threatened to make war against France, unless the French people placed Louis upon the throne again. It does not seem as if the allies, as they were called, had much right to interfere between the French people and their King. But perhaps they feared that their own people might follow the example of the French if they did not do something.

At first Britain did not openly join with the others. But in January 1793 the French put their King to death, and a few weeks after Britain joined the allies.

If you look on the map you will see how many other lands border on France, and what a great frontier, as the part of one country which borders on another is called, the French had to protect. In the north they were attacked by British, Dutch, and Austrians—for Austria had at that time possession of the Netherlands. Prussians and the Princes of the Empire attacked them along the Upper Rhine; the King of Sardinia at the Piedmontese Alps; the King of Spain in the passes of the Pyrenees. Switzerland only, of all the countries bordering upon France, had not joined the allies. But some of the French themselves joined them, so that France had to fight a civil war as well.

Among the French who helped the allies and who were helped by them were the people of Toulon. An army of British, Spaniards, and Neapolitans took possession of the fortress, and a squadron of British ships lay in the harbour.

Toulon is a fine natural harbour on the Mediterranean. It is a strong fortress lying at the head of a deep double bay, and after Brest is the most important arsenal and naval port in France. Although it has a commercial harbour too, it is not of commercial importance like Marseilles, but is used almost entirely by the French navy. It is a good place for a naval station, as the bay is well sheltered and the anchorage good. There are shipbuilding yards and graving docks here, as coal and iron can easily be brought from the mines in the Department Gard, and from Ardèche, and even from Isère.

The other two greatest naval stations of France are Brest and Cherbourg. But they both lie on the northern shore. The south coast of France is cut off, as it were, from the north and west by the Iberian Peninsula, as Spain and Portugal are called. The Mediterranean shore can only be reached through the Straits of Gibraltar, and the fortress of Gibraltar belongs to the British, so you can see how important it was for France that Toulon should be recovered. At this time, too, Toulon was thought to be one of the strongest fortresses in the world, and the command of it meant, to a great extent, the command of the Mediterranean.

The French revolutionary army, however, at Toulon was badly officered, and the soldiers were almost without discipline. For the revolution which had begun in a demand for liberty and justice from an oppressed people had grown into a horrible war of class hatred. The people had suffered so much from the nobles that, now that they had them in their power, their hatred knew no bounds. Hundreds of nobles were put to death for the simple reason that they were noble. No one who had rank or authority was safe, and France ran red with blood.

The people declared that there should be no more nobles, and no more titles, but all were to be equal. Even "Madame" and "Monsieur," which mean the same as our "Mr." and "Mrs.," were not allowed to be used. Every one was addressed alike as "citizen" or "citizeness."

In the slaughter of nobles, many of the officers of the army had been killed. Others had fled from the country to save their lives. So it came about that men with no knowledge of how to command became officers, and the soldiers, who were told that all men were equal, were, on their side, little willing to obey. The commander-in-chief of the army before Toulon was a painter. He could, no doubt, paint fine pictures of battles, but he did not know in the least how to fight them. He was very vain, too, and thought that he was doing great things. He rode about in a splendid uniform covered with gold lace, which showed off his fine figure. He pulled his long moustache and looked very fierce and grand, but was really of no use. Under him he had an army of about ten thousand men, but few of them were real soldiers. Many had joined because they knew that the army was going to sunny Provence, where grapes and figs grew, which they could plunder at will. Some of them had no arms, others did not know how to use them, and every one, high and low, wanted to go his own way.

Such was the state of the army before Toulon when Napoleon arrived there.

CHAPTER IX

THE TAKING OF TOULON

Napoleon was on his way from Avignon to rejoin his regiment at Nice when he came to Toulon. Avignon is an interesting old town on the Rhône. Its streets are narrow and winding, and so swept by wind that it has been called "Avignon the Windy." It has been called "The City of Bells" too, from its many churches and convents. It shares with Rome the honour of having been the seat of the Popes, and for many years both Avignon and the country round belonged to them. Now, like many other towns near, it has silk factories. Napoleon had been sent there to look after some war stores. He arrived at Toulon just after the commander of artillery had been wounded, and the men were without a leader. The post was offered to Citizen Bonaparte, who took it at once.

It is said by some that the taking of Toulon was due to Napoleon, for he at once saw the weakness of the painter-soldier's plans. He saw that, even had the army been well drilled, it was not large enough to surround and really besiege the town. The thing to do was to get possession of a fort within cannon-shot of the British fleet, bombard that, and so cut the town off from their help. "Toulon is there," said Napoleon, putting his finger upon a fort called Eguillette, marked upon the map.

The painter laughed, and nudged the man next him. "Here is a rascal who does not know much about geography," he said.

But what Napoleon meant was that, if that fort were taken, Toulon would fall. The painter did not believe him, and would do nothing to help his new commander of artillery—"Captain Cannon," he called him scornfully.

Other people think that Napoleon has had too much credit for the siege of Toulon, and that his part in it was really very small. However that may be, he seems to have worked very hard. "Do your duty," he said to the other officers, "and let me do mine."

He had need to work, for when he joined the army they had hardly any artillery at all. In a few days he had forty cannon and everything needed for the building of new forts. He gathered shot and shell too, and built forts and batteries. He wrote, ordered, and fought unceasingly.

With all his quickness and eagerness, Napoleon was cool and calm. He admired coolness and calmness in others too. One day in the middle of a fight he wanted to send an order, and called out for some one who could write. A young soldier, called Junot, immediately came forward. As he was leaning against the breastwork of the battery writing, a bullet hit the ground close to him, scattering the earth all over his paper. "Good!" said Junot calmly, "we won't need any sand." In those days, when people had no blotting-paper, they used sand to dry the ink. Napoleon never forgot that young soldier. Later he became a marshal of France and Duke of Abrantes.

One battery which Napoleon had built was in such a dangerous place that few could be found to man it. So Napoleon put up a notice-board bearing the words, "The Battery of Fearless Men." After that all the bravest in the army were eager to serve there.

The painter grumbled at the manner in which Napoleon took things into his own hands, but his wife was more sensible. "Leave the boy alone," she said; "he knows more about it than you do. He does not ask you to do anything. If he wins, the glory will be yours. If he makes mistakes, the fault is his."

At last the painter was recalled. But an old doctor, who had taken to writing novels, was sent in his place, and things did not go much better. "Are we always to have painters and doctors to command us?" grumbled the soldiers.

Then the doctor too was recalled, and a real soldier, named Dugommier, was sent as commander-in-chief. He was eager, quick, knew how to fight, and how to make men obey him. His very look was enough. He was tall and strong, his face was tanned and brown with sun and wind, and from under his thick white hair his eyes shone piercingly. He knew and judged men quickly, and at once he saw that the young officer Napoleon Bonaparte knew what he was about.

For another month the siege went on. There were attacks and counter-attacks, assaults, and sallies, and at last L'Eguillette was taken. "Tomorrow, or the day after, we shall sup in Toulon," said Napoleon.

And he was right. The British ships could not remain under the fire of the French guns, and they made ready to sail away. The people of Toulon were seized with panic. The British ships were their last and only hope. Nothing else could save them from falling into the hands of the terrible revolutionists, so they made ready to go with them. Soon the sea was crowded with boats carrying terror-stricken men, women, and children to the fleet. In their haste many were drowned, sometimes whole boatloads being overturned by the too eager crowds.

All day the flight lasted. Then about nine o'clock in the evening a terrible explosion shook the earth. The sea seemed to belch forth fire, the dark night was suddenly bright as day, and horrible with noise and smoke. Fierce red flames licked the sky, and, black against the lurid light, showed the shattered hulks of ships. It was the British commander who, before leaving, had set fire to a great part of the arsenal and blown up about a dozen French ships of war.

Next day the victorious troops marched into the now almost silent and deserted town. Then began horrible scenes of slaughter. Those who still remained within the walls were shot down by hundreds in cold blood. The victors, mad with revenge, revelled in horrid butchery.

However hardened Napoleon may have become later, he took no part in this. Grave and silent, he looked on at what he had no power to hinder.

CHAPTER X

NAPOLEON'S MARRIAGE

After the siege of Toulon, Napoleon was sent to inspect the forts and defences of the coast of Provence. Soon we find him with the army of Italy, as it was called, fighting against the Piedmontese and the King of Sardinia. Italy at this time was not one United Kingdom as it is now. It was divided into many states, each ruled by a different prince, and Piedmont belonged to the King of Sardinia. These states are all cut off from the rest of Europe, as it were, by the Alps, which are the highest mountains on the Continent. Their steepest sides are turned towards Italy, so that it is easier for an army to pass into Italy than to pass out of it. But the army of Italy was under an officer, who was brave and clever indeed, but so old and ill that he spent much of his time in bed. So although the army lay in strong positions on the hills, the war dragged slowly along, neither side doing much. Soon after Napoleon joined the army, however, the Sardinians were beaten back, and the French gained an entrance into Italy.

Napoleon by this time had made good friends among the men who were ruling France, and it seemed as if his fortune was made. But these were very wild and uncertain times. Soon his friends fell into disgrace, and Napoleon himself was put into prison for a short time. At last we find him once more, poor and lonely, wandering the streets of Paris, with nothing to do. For he had thrown up his commission rather than go to a foot regiment, as he had been ordered to do.

But it was now, when he seemed forgotten and cast aside, that his great chance came to him.

France, besides having to fight outside enemies, was full of unrest and discontent within its borders. The people were tired of the Convention, as the Government was now called, and wished to over-throw its power. At last the citizens of Paris took up arms, and resolved to attack the palace of the Tuileries. The soldiers of the Convention marched to meet the rebels. But when their leader saw the rebels drawn up in fighting order, he marched back again.

The members of the Convention then gathered to consult. They knew that their danger was great. They must do something quickly, if they were not to be overthrown. But who was to lead their soldiers.

Suddenly one of their number called Barras rose. "I know the man whom you want," he said. "He is a little Corsican officer who will not stand on ceremony."

So Napoleon was sent for.

It was by this time late at night. But Napoleon began to work at once, and by six o'clock next morning every street leading to the Tuileries was guarded with cannon.

The rioters had no cannon, but they were well armed with muskets, and thirty thousand of them came crowding along the narrow streets to besiege the palace.

For many hours the two forces stood facing each other, neither exchanging a shot; but at last, about half-past four, some one fired. It was a signal for all to begin. Napoleon's cannon swept the streets. The rioters fled before the hail of grape-shot, leaving their dead upon the ground. By six in the evening all was quiet again. Thanks to "the little Corsican," the Convention had won. And Napoleon had gained for himself the post of commander-in-chief of the army of the Interior.

But although the Convention had won for the moment, Paris was by no means quieted. So Napoleon had his hands full.

The Government was now called the Directory, although it

The little Corsican Officer

was little changed from the Convention. The people were still starving, bread was scarce, and riots frequent.

Sometimes Napoleon would try to quiet the people by talking to them. Once, when he had nearly succeeded in making them go away peaceably, a big fat woman in the crowd cried out, "Don't listen to him. These fine officers, with their gold lace and epaulettes, don't care who starves so long as they have plenty to eat and grow fat upon."

"My good woman," replied Napoleon quickly, "look at me and look at yourself, and then tell me which is the fattest." And as Napoleon was very small and thin, the fat woman had to laugh. The crowd laughed with her, and so they scattered in good humour.

One day very soon after Napoleon had been made commander-in-chief, a boy of about twelve asked to see him. The boy's name was Eugène Beauharnais, and with tears in his eyes he told Napoleon that his father had been a soldier. He had fought for the republic, but had been killed among many others, because he was a noble. Now Eugène came to beg for his father's sword.

Napoleon was sorry for the boy, and ordered at once that the sword should be given to him. As soon as Eugène saw it he seized it, kissed it, and carried it away happy.

The next day, Eugène's mother, who was a very beautiful lady, came to thank Napoleon for having been so kind to her boy. Very soon Napoleon began to love this beautiful lady, although she was many years older than he. She loved him too, and in a short time they were married.

So in a few short months, from being almost penniless and unknown, Napoleon had become famous and well off, and had married a great lady, who was able to make friends for him among the rulers of the land.

CHAPTER XI

NAPOLEON PASSES THE ALPS

Josephine de Beauharnais had married a great man, or rather, a man who was going to be great, and a few days after the wedding they had to say good-bye to each other. For among the Alps there was still fighting, and Napoleon was ordered off to take command of the army of Italy.

"You are too young," said a member of the Directory doubtfully.

"In a year I shall either have Milan or be dead," replied Napoleon, smiling. Milan is the capital of Lombardy, but the words "mille ans," pronounced almost the same, mean, in French, "a thousand years."

When Napoleon reached the army of Italy, he found it in a very bad condition. The men were in rags and almost starving. They had hardly any cavalry, no baggage horses of any kind, and no money with which to buy any. They had only thirty cannon, and no powder or shot. Against this beggared and hungry army were arrayed eighty thousand men, with more than two hundred cannon.

Napoleon made up his mind that his soldiers should no longer sit still and starve. Across the rugged Alps lay the fertile plains of Piedmont and Lombardy. Into these fertile plains Napoleon resolved to carry the war. "Soldiers," he said to his men, "you are starving and almost naked. The Government owes you much, and has nothing to give you. Your patience and courage do you honour, but they have brought you neither glory nor any other good. But I will lead you into the most fertile plains in all the world. There you will find great towns and rich lands. There you will find honour, glory, and wealth. Soldiers of the army of Italy, do you lack courage?"

These words, spoken by a commander who seemed little more than a boy to men who themselves were nearly all young, and who were eager for adventure, who had fame to win, and nothing to lose, were received with cheers. Never before had the soldiers been spoken to in such a way. They had been told of tyrants to be overthrown, of liberty to be won, of chains to be broken. But now the glitter of gold and the hope of gain was held before their eyes, and they marched eagerly behind such a leader. Their battles were no longer to be battles for freedom, but for conquest.

When Napoleon first took command of the army of Italy he was at Nice. Nice is the chief town of the department of Alpes Maritimes, and lies upon the shores of the Mediterranean, sheltered on the north, north-east, and north-west by hills which slope ridge behind ridge to the Maritime Alps, from which the department takes its name. Being so sheltered, its climate is mild, and during the winter people flock there from all the cold and wet parts of Europe, and especially from the British Isles, in search of warmth and sunshine. From Nice in France, to Spezia in Italy, the coast land is called the Riviera. Between Nice and Genoa it is called the Riviera di Ponente. Between Genoa and Spezia it is called the Riviera di Levante. And all along, among beautiful scenery and under sunny skies, are towns and villages, which, although many of them are engaged in the manufacture of olive oil, silk, and perfumes, get their greatest wealth from the numbers of visitors who flock there every year.

The Alps guard all the landward borders of Italy. To cross them, Napoleon knew, would be a matter of great difficulty and danger, for the enemy watched the passes well. So he made up his mind not to cross, but to round the mountains.

Above the Gulf of Genoa, where the Alps curve round the coast, they begin to slope away. Here, too, the Apennines, which run right down the long "leg" of Italy, begin to rise. And between these two ranges is the only spot by which Italy can be reached without crossing high mountains. By this way Napoleon decided to lead his men.

It will not be possible to follow Napoleon through all his battles. He had to fight two armies—one Austrian and one Sardinian. Against so strong an enemy he knew that his only hope was in quick marches and surprises. He must surround and astonish the foe, and take him at a disadvantage. To do this his own army must travel without baggage, so as to be able to move quickly, and his men must trust to finding all they needed for food and clothes in the country to which they went.

Napoleon knew that if the two armies of his enemies joined and attacked him together, they would be too strong for him. So he tried to keep them apart, and fight first one and then the other. This he succeeded in doing.

The Sardinian army was the first to be crushed. Not without much fighting did the French cross the hills behind Genoa and Savona, and at last reach the heights, and look down upon the plain, of Piedmont. It was a splendid sight. The one great river of Italy, the Po, rolled through the plain, with its hundreds of tributaries twining in and out among vineyards, rice and maize fields, groves of mulberry trees, and rich meadows, where the crop grows so fast that it may be reaped from four to nine times in the year. And far away beyond this fertile plain rose the snowy boundary of the Alps. The great gate of Italy had opened as by a magic word to the conqueror. "Hannibal forced the Alps," cried Napoleon "we have turned them."

And as the soldiers gazed upon the beautiful sight they cheered their young leader, for already Napoleon had begun to fill his men with that love for him and eagerness to follow him which made him victorious upon a hundred battlefields.

CHAPTER XII

IN THE GREAT PLAIN OF ITALY

The Po, the largest river of Italy, rises on Mont Viso, one of the Cottian Alps, at more than six thousand feet above sea level, and to begin with is but a mountain stream. From its source to where it enters the plain at Revello is only twenty-one miles, but during these twenty-one miles it rushes and tumbles down more than five thousand feet. From Revello it flows on quickly through the plain, becoming broader and broader until, when it reaches Turin, it is a great river, upon which ships may sail all the three hundred miles to its mouth in the Adriatic.

Below Pavia it is joined by a great tributary called the Ticino, and further on by the Adda, both of which are navigable right up to the beautiful lakes Maggiore and Como, out of which they flow. From Piacenza onward, the Po flows very slowly. Indeed the fall of the land to the coast is so slight that the Po would not flow at all were it not for the rushing mountain streams which pour into it.

These mountain streams make the river very muddy, for they bring a great deal of soil down from the mountain-sides. This has become much worse lately, for the trees on the hillsides have been recklessly cut down, and no others planted to take their place. The roots of trees help to hold the moisture and keep the soil together, but when this protection is gone, the earth is much more easily washed away, and many places that were once green mountain pastures have become barren rocks.

As the river flows so slowly, much of this mud brought down from the mountains is deposited in the river bed. So the bed rises higher and higher, until now it is really higher than the surrounding plain. And from Piacenza to the sea, great dykes have been built all along its banks, to keep it from overflowing the surrounding country. These dykes were begun before the time of the Romans, but they have still to be watched, added to, and altered, as the bed of the river changes.

Italy is a land of sunshine, and the air is dry. Yet the land is fertile, for the rivers, though not of much good for trade, are good for watering the land. You will see from the map how the whole northern plain is crossed and re-crossed by streams. These streams are fed by the heavy rains which fall in the Alps and Apennines. For high mountains always catch the rain-clouds as they blow across the land. They are also fed by the melting in summer of the eternal snows upon the Alps. And of course the hotter the summer sun, the more snow is melted, and comes down in torrents to the valley below.

Upon the slopes of the mountains (Piedmont means "the foot of the mountain") many sheep are fed. And this has led to wool factories being set up at Turin—this and the supply of mountain streams. For Italy has hardly any coal, and a country which has to import coal cannot become a great manufacturing country unless there is a good supply of water-power. And then factories can only be set up where there is water-power. Its lack of coal, its climate, and fine soil have made Italy not a manufacturing, but an agricultural country. Besides this, the scenery of Italy is so beautiful, it has so many towns full of splendid buildings, of pictures and sculpture, it has so much history, and so many of the great things of the world have happened there, that every year many visitors go to it from other lands. In this way much money is brought to the country, and we may be glad, perhaps, that Italy has no coal, and that one of the most beautiful countries of the world cannot be spoiled by smoky factories.

Now Napoleon marched victoriously through Piedmont, and

in a few weeks he lay not far from Turin, the capital. It is a busy, prosperous town, with wide streets and beautiful houses. Lying near the head of the plain, it commands the trade passing through the great Mont Cenis Tunnel. This tunnel, which is nearly eight miles long, was pierced through the Alps, so that both people and goods can pass quickly by train, instead of slowly over the road, as in the days of Napoleon.

At Mondovi there had been a battle in which Napoleon had beaten the Sardinians so thoroughly that their King was eager to make peace, and so save his capital, Turin, from destruction. And at Cherasco, about thirty or forty miles from Turin, the peace was signed. By this treaty the King gave up most of his fortresses. It put all the roads leading into France into Napoleon's hands, and so, with the country safe behind him, left him free to march into Lombardy against the Austrians.

The poor King of Sardinia was shorn of nearly all his power. He was, indeed, allowed to keep his throne and crown, but he felt that he had been conquered and humiliated, and he became so sad that it was not long before he died.

CHAPTER XIII

THE LITTLE CORPORAL

Napoleon now invaded Lombardy. In order to reach Milan he had to cross the Po. He knew that this would be hard to do, in the face of a watchful foe. So, while he really meant to cross at Piacenza, he pretended to be going to cross at Valenza, about fifty miles farther up, where the Austrian leader awaited him. Having thoroughly deceived the Austrians, he marched quickly to Piacenza. The river here is nearly a quarter of a mile broad, and the ferry-boat could only carry five hundred men at a time, and took half-an-hour to cross. But so skilfully did Napoleon manage, that his army was safely over before the Austrian leader discovered that he had been deceived.

Napoleon now marched on Milan. As he marched through Parma, another of the states into which Italy was divided, the Duke sent messengers begging for peace. This Napoleon granted on condition that the Duke paid a large sum of money, gave stores and horses for the army, and sent twenty fine pictures to France.

Italy is a land of art. It is full of fine pictures and sculptures. Napoleon thought that he would like to get some of these for France. So now he began a system, which he carried on through all his wars, of making the conquered people give some of their art treasures to France. Such a thing had never been done before, at least in modern warfare, and now it caused a great outcry in all Europe. But that did not stop Napoleon, and from now onward he began to gather the treasures of art which made the Louvre one of the finest galleries in the world.

To reach Milan, Napoleon had yet to cross the river Adda. Near

Napoleon at Lodi

the town of Lodi there was a wooden bridge, and here Napoleon decided to cross. But the banks were guarded by the whole Austrian army, and the bridge was swept by their cannon.

Napoleon, placing his cannon opposite that of the enemy, sent his cavalry farther down the stream, to cross by a ford. Meantime he opened fire, and began to rain shot and shell upon the enemy. In the midst of this, his cavalry suddenly appeared on the other side. The Austrians wavered. Then, shouting "Long live the Republic!" the French charged the bridge. But such a terrible fire met them that they too wavered. Then Napoleon himself seized a standard and urged them onward. The bridge was passed. Right up to the enemy's guns they charged. The gunners died at their posts, but the Austrians were scattered, and fled in utter confusion, chased by the French, until darkness ended the flight and slaughter.

Napoleon himself called it "the terrible passage of Lodi." The French only lost about two hundred men, the Austrians ten times as many. After this battle the French were so delighted with their clever leader that they called him the "Little Corporal," which for many a day was his name among his soldiers.

The road to Milan now lay open, and a few days later Napoleon entered the city in triumph.

Milan is now one of the richest commercial and manufacturing cities of Italy. It lies in the centre of the fertile plain of Lombardy, upon a navigable river called the Olona, and by canals and waterways it is connected with Lakes Maggiore and Como and with the sea. It also commands the railway line which leads northward through the St. Gothard Tunnel, so that it has plenty of outlet for its commerce, which has greatly increased since the tunnel was opened.

The St. Gothard Tunnel is more than nine miles long, and through it thunder trains laden not only with finished goods, but with much raw silk from the mulberry trees of Lombardy, to the silk-mills of Switzerland and Alsace.

Besides its silk trade, which is its greatest, Milan has woollen and glove factories, supplied by the sheep pastures; cutlery, and machinery even, for iron is found in the plains of Lombardy. It also exports butter, eggs, cheese, and poultry. The two most famous cheeses of Italy—Gorgonzola and Parmesan—come from here.

But this busy town, as big as our smoky Manchester, is beautiful too. Like all the great towns of Italy, it has played a part in the history of the world. In the time of the Romans it was one of the great cities of the empire. Its streets are still full of beautiful buildings. Its great cathedral is one of the largest and most splendid in the world, its school of singing the most famous of Europe. Its galleries are filled with fine pictures and priceless art treasures.

Of these fine pictures Napoleon now claimed twenty for France.

CHAPTER XIV

ABOUT SOME OF THE TOWNS WHICH NAPOLEON SAW IN ITALY

The people of Milan opened their gates to Napoleon, and even welcomed him as a deliverer. For the Italians did not love their Austrian rulers, and Napoleon made them believe that he had come to free them. But the fortress held out against him, and leaving some soldiers to take it, he marched on to Mantua.

As the conqueror advanced, the Austrian army fell back beyond the river Adige, leaving a garrison in Mantua. The war had now reached the borders of the Republic of Venice. Venice was at peace with France, but that did not prevent Napoleon taking possession of Verona, one of the most important and beautiful towns of Venetia. For by so doing he commanded the passes into Tyrol, and made it difficult for fresh troops to reach the Austrian army.

Verona is a university town. It is also a strong fortress and headquarters of part of the Italian army. But perhaps to us it is most interesting as the place where Romeo and Juliet, whom Shakespeare tells us about, lived. Juliet's house is still pointed out.

While he besieged Mantua, Napoleon sent another part of his army to subdue Genoa, which is the chief commercial town of Italy. It forms the main outlet on the western side for the fertile plains of Piedmont and Lombardy. For although it seems to lie on the wrong side of the Alps for that, it has good communications inland over much the same route as Napoleon took. Indeed, so low are the hills that at one time it was intended to connect the Adriatic and the Mediterranean by canals and waterways, by means of the rivers Bormido, Tanaro, and Po.

Besides being a commercial town, Genoa is a strong fortress and headquarters of part of the Italian army. It is called "the Superb," and it seems to rise straight out of the sea, and to be crowned with splendid palaces. It was most important for Napoleon to gain possession of Genoa, so that troops coming from France might pass safely into Lombardy.

Napoleon himself marched through Italy to Piacenza, Parma, Reggio, Modena, and at last to Bologna.

By this time nearly all the north of Italy was in his power. In the south the Kings of Naples and Sicily had made peace with him. There only remained the Papal States. Bologna formed part of the Papal States, but the people were discontented, and welcomed Napoleon gladly. The Pope began to fear the loss of his state, so he sent a messenger to Napoleon, who made peace, for the time at least, on condition that the Pope gave him food, money, and horses for his army, and a hundred works of art for France. Bologna, Ferrara, and Ancona were also to be given up to the French.

Bologna is called "the Learned," and has an ancient and famous university, the oldest in Europe. It is now also an important commercial town and railway junction, with linen factories, supplied with hemp from the plains around, and with water-power from the slopes of the Apennines, upon which it stands.

From Bologna Napoleon crossed the Apennines to Pistoia in Tuscany. Pistoia has gun factories, and it is said that pistols were first made here, and so got their name. Tuscany has more minerals than any other part of Italy, and iron is also imported from the island of Elba, which lies only six miles from the shore, and which has been always famous for its ore. Even in the time of the Romans Tuscany was famous for its bronze.

Napoleon next marched to Leghorn, which, after Genoa, is the most important seaport in Italy. He hoped to seize some British ships there; they had been warned in time, however, and had gone. But they had left goods behind them worth £475,000, which Napoleon seized for the use of his army.

Being so near Elba, Leghorn has a shipbuilding yard and an iron foundry. It also does great trade in silk, cotton, and wool, and has a grain and petroleum trade with the Black Sea.

From Leghorn Napoleon went back to Florence, the capital of Tuscany, to visit the Grand Duke. He was the brother of the Emperor, but as yet was at peace with France.

Florence, "the Beautiful," is situated in a rich and fertile valley, and is one of the most interesting cities of Italy. It is a city of art, and it is to Florence that modern Italy owes much of its art and literature. Here Dante was born, Boccaccio lived, Savonarola preached and died. Among its many painters were Leonardo da Vinci, Michael Angelo, and Raphael; among its wise men Machiavelli and Galileo.

So Florence is full of memories. Its streets are lined with splendid palaces; and its treasures of art, its pictures and sculptures, are priceless.

CHAPTER XV

MANTUA AND VENICE

While Napoleon was at Florence, he heard that the fortress of Milan had yielded, and having secured peace in the rest of Italy, he was able to turn all his attention to the taking of Mantua. The Austrian leader, Beaulieu, having lost so many battles, had been recalled by the Emperor, and now an old general, called Marshal Würmser, came marching against the French with many fresh soldiers.

But this new army and new general fared little better than the old. Napoleon, however, had now so few soldiers that he had not enough to besiege Mantua and fight against Würmser too. So he was obliged to raise the siege, and gather all his men to meet the old general. Again, in battle after battle, the Austrians were defeated. The French army marched here and there with such speed as could hardly be believed. Napoleon himself shared all the hardships of his men, glad at times to eat dry bread for his supper, and often sleeping upon the field. At last the campaign was over, and Würmser was shut up in Mantua, with twenty-six thousand men.

Except as a fortress, Mantua is not a town of great importance. It was very unhealthy, being built on islands and surrounded on all sides by marshy ground, and by lakes made by the river Mincio. But, being so surrounded, it formed a splendid natural fortress. It could only be reached by five paths, which were defended by forts, gates, and drawbridges.

While this second siege of Mantua was going on, the Austrians sent another army against the French. But it was chiefly raw recruits, and Napoleon beat them, as he had beaten all the others.

For more than four months the Austrians in Mantua held out. Many of the men fell ill from the foul airs which rose from the swamps around, many died. Food grew scarcer and scarcer, till everything, even to horses, was eaten. At last, worn out by hunger and disease, old Würmser gave in.

After the fall of Mantua, Napoleon marched southwards against his last remaining enemy in Italy—the Pope. As the conqueror marched, the people fled before him. Battles he fought and won, and after nine days' war the Pope was glad to make peace. He gave up to the French conqueror all but a mere pretence of worldly power. For ages the word of the Pope had made kings, and princes, and whole nations tremble. From now onward his power became but a shadow of his former greatness.

But although the Austrians were now driven out of Italy, they were by no means crushed, and Napoleon next prepared to march into Austria, to fight there. The Austrians had gathered another army, under the Archduke Charles, who, like Napoleon, was young and successful. He had already beaten the French where they had been fighting on the borders of the Rhine, and it was now hoped that he would beat Napoleon.

Like Italy, Austria-Hungary is a land of mountains. Like Italy, it has one great plain, the plain of Hungary, which is surrounded by high mountains, of which the Carpathians and the Alps are the chief. Like Italy, it has one great river, the Danube. But unlike Italy, which has a great deal of sea-coast, it has very little. And that little, although very ragged and beset with many islands, has only three good ports—Trieste, Fiume, and Pola. Having so little coast, and being so surrounded by mountains, the climate of Austria-Hungary is very dry. The extremes of heat and cold are also strongly marked, for when water surrounds a country it keeps the air at a more even temperature than when land surrounds it. The dry air of Austria is not only good for growing wheat, but for grinding it into flour. If you buy flour, and ask for Hungarian flour, you will find that it is the dearest kind. But it is so light and fine that it is considered best for making cakes and light pastries.

Unlike Italy, too, Austria has plenty of coal and iron, so it is a manufacturing country, although most of the people earn their living by farming.

It was in the mountains of Austria, on the borders of Tyrol, and in the mountains of Carinthia and Styria, that the war now went on. But there, as in the plains of Italy, Napoleon conquered. Trieste and Fiume were in his hands, and he himself was marching upon Vienna, the capital, when the Emperor made peace.

First a treaty, called the treaty of Leoben, from the name of the town in Austria where it was signed, was agreed upon. Later came another, called the treaty of Campo-Formio. By this treaty Napoleon made the first of those changes in the map of Europe for which he was soon to be famous. Belgium and the Austrian Netherlands, as they were then called, with Corfu and the Ionian Islands, were given to France. The north of Italy was formed into the Cis-Alpine Republic, but was really under France, and to make up somewhat for the loss of these possessions, Austria was given Venetia—that is, all the part of the northern plain of Italy which lies along the coast from Verona to the Gulf of Trieste.

Venetia had been a neutral state—that is, its people had taken neither one side nor the other. But it was hard to be neutral where Napoleon was concerned. He could see only friends or enemies. He made Venice an enemy, conquered it, and handed it over to another state. So Venice, the beautiful bride of the sea, with all her landward possessions, lost her freedom.

Venice, which is called the "Bride of the Sea" and "Queen of the Adriatic," seems to rise straight out of it. Its marble palaces are built upon a hundred islands. Here there is neither dust nor din, as in other cities, for the streets are canals, and the carriages small black boats, called gondolas. These move along swiftly and silently, the rower, who stands to row, uttering strange cries as he rounds the corners, to warn others who may be coming in opposite directions. Over the canals there are many bridges, and by the side numberless little lanes and pathways, for those who wish to walk from place to place.

As a place of trade, Venice has a great history. In the fifteenth century it was a city of powerful merchants and was the heart of European trade, and its flag was respected on every sea. But when Napoleon invaded it, Venice had lost nearly all its old importance. But now it flourishes again, and is Italy's greatest seaport on the eastern side. Much of the trade of Lombardy passes through it. It is also a naval port, and arsenal, with shipbuilding and torpedo works. But perhaps it is most widely known for the manufacture of beautiful coloured glass, which we call Venetian glass.

CHAPTER XVI

NAPOLEON RETURNS TO FRANCE

Napoleon, in all his fighting in Italy, did not act merely as a commander and soldier. He acted more like a conqueror and ruler. It seemed as if he were not working for the Republic of France, but for himself. He did as he liked. "Do you suppose," he said, "that I triumph in Italy for the glory of the lawyers of the Directory? Do you suppose I mean to found a republic? What an idea! The nation wants a chief, a chief covered with glory."

He had covered himself with glory. His soldiers, whom he led with such splendid success, with such skill and daring, loved him, forgetting the many of their comrades who had died that they might conquer. Yet the discipline in his army was severe, the order perfect. It was because he both blamed sternly and rewarded well that his men loved him. Once, when a division had given way before the enemy, he said to them, "Soldiers, I am not pleased with you. You have shown neither discipline nor pluck. You have allowed yourselves to be driven from a position that a handful of brave men would have held against an army. Major, write on their flag, 'They do not belong to the army of Italy.'" And the men, with tears in their eyes, begged for another chance.

Yet, another time, after a long day's march, finding a sentinel asleep at his post, Napoleon quietly took his place for him. Suddenly the man awoke, and seeing who was standing sentry, fell upon his knees in terror, begging forgiveness. "Friend," replied Napoleon, "you had fought hard and marched far. I happened to be awake, and took your post. Another time you will be more careful." It was little wonder that the men loved the leader of whom such stories were told.

Napoleon had promised his men a fruitful land to plunder. But when they took him at his word and plundered, they were punished. But he himself was the arch-plunderer, and his men did not lack rewards. "I am the enemy of tyrants," he said, who was himself a tyrant; "but before all I am the enemy of rogues, robbers, and anarchists. I shoot my soldiers when they pillage." Napoleon's robbery was robbery with order and method, and through it all he pretended to be the friend and deliverer of Italy. It was hard, however, for the Italians to believe in a friend who robbed them. But when they rose against him he called it rebellion, and crushed them.

While the treaty of Campo-Formio was being drawn up, Napoleon held court with great state at the castle of Montebello near Milan. It was like the court of a king, and when Josephine, his beautiful wife, joined him here, she moved like a queen amid the glittering crowds. For to Montebello came messengers from the courts of nearly all Europe—from the Emperor, from the Kings of Naples and Sardinia, from the Pope, and from many lesser princes and rulers.

After the treaty was quite settled, Napoleon said good-bye to his soldiers, and set out for Paris. "Soldiers," he said, "I set out to-morrow. Far from my army, I shall comfort myself with the hope of being soon with you again, ready to fight fresh dangers. Soldiers, when you talk of the princes you have conquered, of the nations you have set free, and the battles you have fought in two campaigns, say, 'In the next we shall do still more.'"

When Napoleon arrived, the people of Paris greeted him eagerly, and thronged to see him. They changed the name of the street in which he lived to Victory Street. But the rulers, the Directory, had begun to be afraid of this imperious soldier, who looked so small and delicate, and who had yet a will of iron, and seemed to hold the fate of nations in his hand. They were jealous of him, too, for wherever he went, it was the conqueror of Italy who was cheered, not the rulers of France. And every soldier declared that it was high time to be done with lawyers, and make the "Little Corporal" king.

Some new work had to be found for the "Little Corporal" and his restless brain. France and Britain were at this time bitter enemies, and the French were eager to conquer Britain. So Napoleon was now made commander-in-chief of the army of England, as it was called.

He went to Brest, Cherbourg, Le Havre, Dieppe, Boulogne, Calais, Dunkerque - to all the ports along the coast of France opposite England. There he inspected the fortresses, the ships, the soldiers and sailors, gathered for the great attack. But Napoleon saw clearly that France was not yet strong enough upon the sea to attack Britain directly. So he decided to carry out another plan which he had long thought of. That was to conquer Egypt, to found a colony there, and thus in some way injure Britain's trade with India and the East.

Egypt at this time was claimed by the Turks, and formed part of the Ottoman Empire. France and Turkey were at peace, but that made little difference to Napoleon.

The Directory agreed to Napoleon's plan for conquering Egypt. They were very anxious to get the better of Britain in some way, and they were not a little anxious to get rid of Napoleon, and keep him busy at something away from France. So while British ships were watching the northern ports, great and secret preparations were made at Toulon.

CHAPTER XVII

NAPOLEON SETS OUT FOR EGYPT

For his expedition into Egypt Napoleon gathered together about twenty thousand of his finest soldiers and cleverest officers. Besides that he took with him a hundred learned men, painters, and sculptors. For as he had brought back pictures and art treasures from Italy, he meant to bring back treasure of ancient learning from Egypt, and these clever men he took with him to help him. It was perhaps the first time since the days of Alexander the Great that an army had been accompanied by such people.

Although the preparations were made with great secrecy, the British Government learned that something was going on at Toulon. So Nelson was sent with some ships to watch the Mediterranean. But in May, when the French ships were ready to sail, a great storm arose. It did such damage to the British ships that Nelson was obliged to put into a port on the island of Sardinia to have them mended.

Sardinia lies in the Mediterranean, just south of Napoleon's old home, Corsica, and separated from it only by the Strait of Bonifacio. Like Corsica, it is very mountainous. It has a fertile soil and good fisheries. It has valuable minerals too, but they are not much worked.

As soon as Napoleon knew that the way was clear he gave orders to sail. So, on a beautiful May morning, just as the sun was rising, the great fleet sailed out on the waters of the Mediterranean. "Soldiers," said Napoleon to them as they set out, "you are

EUROPE
To Illustrate
"Through Europe with Napoleon."
English Miles.
0 100 200 300 400 500
60
50
40
ATLANTIC OCEAN
BRITISH ISLANDS
SCOTLAND
IRELAND
ENGLAND
LONDON
NORTH SEA
NORWAY
SWEDEN
CHRISTIANIA
STOCKHOLM
DENMARK
BALTIC SEA
Vistula
Hamburg
BERLIN
Elbe
HOLLAND
BELGIUM
BRUSSELS
GERMANY
Frankfurt
Prague
Brest
Seine
PARIS
Loire
Rhine
BAY OF BISCAY
FRANCE
Munich
VIENNA
BUDA-PEST
SWITZERLAND
AUSTRIA
Lyons
Rhône
Venice
Trieste
Turin
Po
Corunna
Oviedo
Oporto
Douro
Astorga
Salamanca
Segovia
MADRID
PORTUGAL
SPAIN
Ebro
Pyrenees
Marseilles
Toulon
Corsica
Ajaccio
ITALY
ADRIATIC SEA
SER
LISBON
Tagus
Talavera
Guadiana
Guadalquiver
Bailen
Seville
ROME
Naples
Str. of Gibraltar
Gibraltar
Sardinia
MEDITERRANEAN
Corfu
Ionian Is.
Sicily
Malta
Valetta
ALGIERS
ALGERIA
TUNIS
ST. HELENA
James Town
Diana Pk.
English Miles
0 5 10

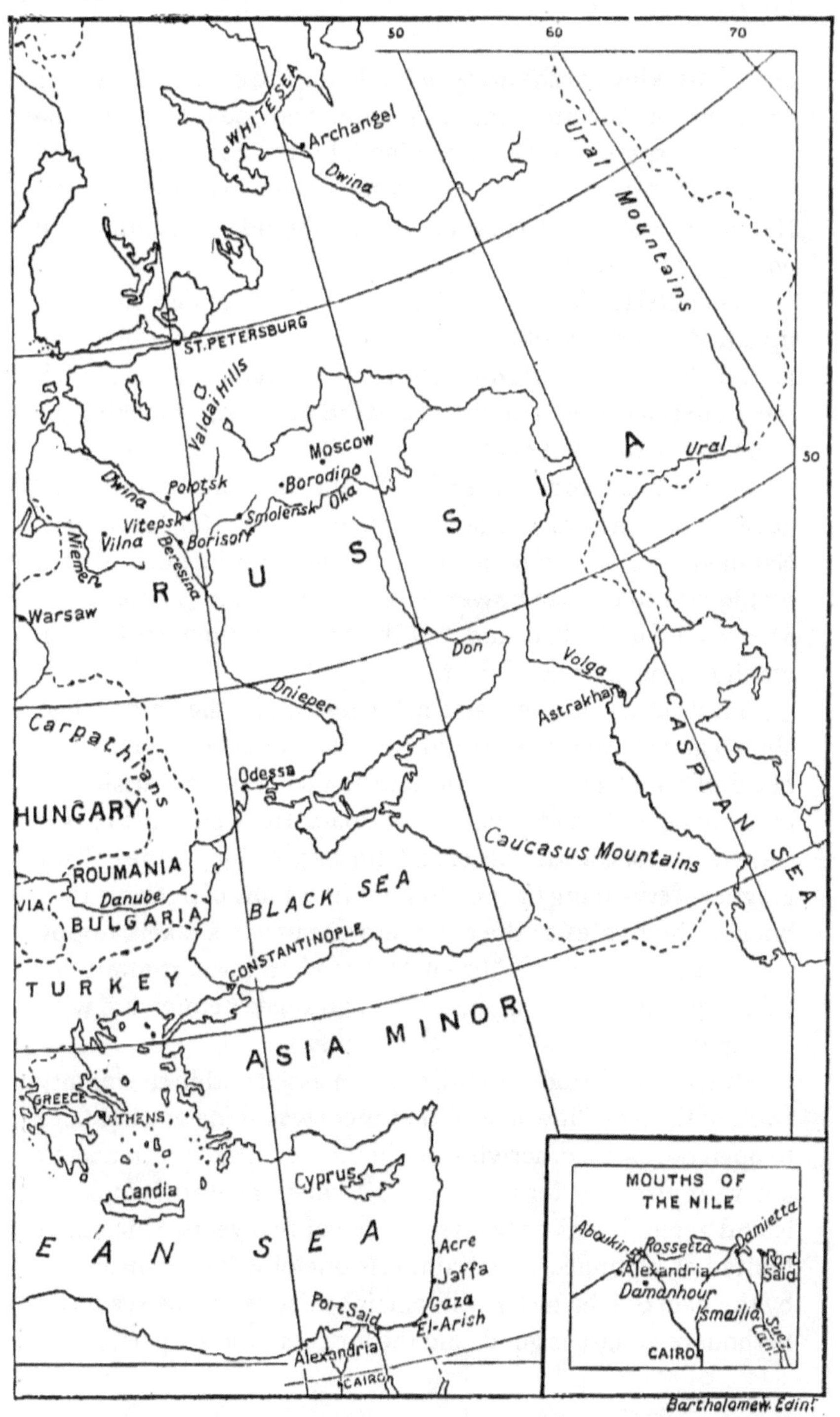

50
60
70
50
WHITE SEA
Archangel
Dwina
Ural Mountains
ST. PETERSBURG
Valdai Hills
Moscow
Borodino
Dwina
Polotsk
Smolensk
Oka
Vitepsk
Borisov
Vilna
Beresina
Niemen
R U S S I A
Warsaw
Ural
Don
Volga
Astrakhan
Dnieper
C A S P I A N   S E A
Carpathians
Odessa
HUNGARY
ROUMANIA
Caucasus Mountains
Danube
BLACK SEA
BULGARIA
VIA
CONSTANTINOPLE
T U R K E Y
ASIA MINOR
GREECE
ATHENS
Cyprus
Candia
E A N   S E A
Acre
Jaffa
Port Said
Gaza
El-Arish
Alexandria
CAIRO
MOUTHS OF
THE NILE
Aboukir
Rossetta
Damietta
Alexandria
Port Said
Damanhour
Ismailia
Suez Canal
CAIRO
Bartholomew, Edin.

one of the wings of the army of England. The eyes of all Europe are upon you. You are going to do more than you have ever done for the prosperity of your fatherland, for the good of man, and for your own glory." Besides speaking to them in this grand way, Napoleon promised each man that he should come home rich enough to buy six acres of land.

When Nelson found that Napoleon had left Toulon, he sailed up and down the Mediterranean looking for him, but he could not find him. For one thing, Nelson still thought that the French meant to sail towards England, and did not think of looking for them on the road to Egypt.

Meanwhile Napoleon reached Malta. Malta at this time was governed by the Knights of St. John, under the King of Naples. Napoleon was very anxious to take Malta, for he knew that it would add to the sea power of whatever nation possessed it. Months before he had said, "With Malta, Sardinia, and Corfu, we should be masters of the Mediterranean."

But Valetta was a very strong fortress, and if the Knights had shown any resistance, it would have cost Napoleon a great deal of trouble, and a great deal of time, to take. With a British fleet cruising near, he had little time to spare. He needed little, as it turned out, for the Knights of St. John were no longer the gallant knights of crusading times. After hardly a show of fighting, they opened their gates to the conqueror. Malta was taken, not by force, but by treachery. "I took Malta when I was at Mantua," said Napoleon, meaning that he had arranged beforehand with the Knights.

"It was well," said a friend, as they passed within the mighty walls of the fort, "it was well that there was some one in Malta to open the gates, otherwise we should never have been able to enter." It was true, for later, in 1800, when the British took the island again, it was only after a siege of two years. Since then Malta has belonged to Britain. It is one of Britain's outposts, by the help of which she still remains mistress of the seas. The harbour of Valetta is good, and the fortress, where a garrison of ten thousand British soldiers is always stationed, is one of the strongest in the world.

But meanwhile Napoleon seized all the cannon, powder, arms, and ships, besides all the gold and silver treasure, belonging to the Knights. He broke up their order, banished them from the island, left a garrison of Frenchmen there, and sailed on his way to Egypt.

On the 30th of June the French fleet arrived safely before Alexandria, two days after Nelson had left. For the British sailor was still scouring the sea from Naples to Alexandria and the coast of Syria, looking for Napoleon, once or twice just missing his prey by wonderful mischance.

When Napoleon arrived at Alexandria the sun was setting, a storm was blowing, and such waves were beating upon the shore that it was dangerous to land. But seeing a strange sail in the distance, Napoleon would not wait. He feared that the British were at last upon his heels. "Fortune," he cried, "I ask but five hours. Will you deny them?"

And so, in the darkness and the storm, the troops were landed on the shore some miles from Alexandria. But the waves were so fierce that many of the men were drowned.

Then through the night the French marched to Alexandria. As day dawned they saw Pompey's Pillar towering over the walls of the city. This is a great column of red granite eighty-nine feet high, which was supposed to mark the grave of Pompey the Great, who was killed here in 48 B.C. But it was really built more than three hundred years later as a landmark for sailors. It was the first of many strange sights which the French soldiers were to see in this new land. "Soldiers," Napoleon had said, "you are going to undertake a conquest the effects of which on civilisation and the trade of the world you cannot know. You are going to strike at Britain a most sure and fatal blow, which we will follow by the deathblow. The first town we shall see was built by Alexander. At every step we will find memories which will make Frenchmen eager to do likewise."

Now, wearied and hungry as they were, the men attacked

Alexandria in the dawning of the day. The Turks and Arabs shut their gates and fought with all their might against this unexpected enemy. But the ancient walls could not stand the onslaught of Napoleon and his legions, and soon the flag of France was floating from the battlements.

CHAPTER XVIII

THE MAMELUKES

Within a week Napoleon had taken Rossetta and Damanhour, two towns near. Damanhour is not of much importance, but Rossetta is interesting. For here one of Napoleon's men found and brought home the Rossetta Stone, which is now in the British Museum. Upon this stone there is writing in three languages. First there is the ancient Egyptian language in hieroglyphics—that is, in figures of birds, beasts, and other things; next there is a much later Egyptian language in writing, and last there is Greek. All these three writings say the same thing over again, and when this was found out, this stone formed a key by which people have since been able to read much that is written in the ancient Egyptian language of hieroglyphics.

Rossetta is also interesting as it is at one of the mouths of the great river Nile. A little below Cairo the Nile divides into two branches. One flows north-east, and the other north-west, and both fall into the Mediterranean more than a hundred miles apart. When a river divides like this it is called a delta, because it forms a shape like the Greek letter Δ, pronounced "delta."

The delta of the Nile is the most fertile and most important part of Egypt, and its three most important cities are at its three corners—Cairo, which is the capital, is the largest and most important city in the country. It stands just above where the river divides, and all the trade, whether coming into or going out of the Nile valley, must pass through it. Alexandria, which is joined to Rossetta by a ship canal, is the second city. It has a good harbour and is the chief port of Egypt. It principally exports grain, cotton, sugar, and onions, grown upon the banks of the Nile. Damietta, at the eastern mouth of the Nile, is the third city. But it is not nearly as prosperous as it used to be, and many of its houses are in ruins. For since the opening of the Suez Canal much of the trade has gone to Port Said and Ismailia, just as the trade of Rossetta goes now through the ship canal to the port of Alexandria.

The Nile is the second longest river in the world, and it is perhaps the most wonderful. No other river is quite like it. Every year it overflows, leaving, as it falls again, a layer of mud upon its banks. This mud is very fertile, and except for this overflowing, Egypt would be a barren waste, like the Libyan Desert on the one side of it and the Arabian Desert on the other.

As it is, rice, wheat, cotton, maize, sugar-cane, indigo, and many other useful things are grown. Tobacco could very well be grown, but it is forbidden for reasons connected with custom duties.

Egypt has thus been called "the gift of the Nile." And so it is. It is a strip of fertile land, only ten or twelve miles wide, which, but for the Nile, would not exist at all, or rather, would only exist as desert. Egypt cannot become a manufacturing country, for it has neither coal, wood, nor oil for fuel, and all its water is needed for watering the land. To supply the houses with oil, oil-bearing plants are grown, such as sesame, mustard, saffron, &c., and lately some trees have been planted, but these are rather for shade than for wood.

Although when Napoleon landed in Egypt the Turks were supposed to rule the land, they had, in fact, very little power. The power was really in the hands of the Mamelukes. These Mamelukes were a wild and fierce people. Their chiefs were called Beys, and there were always twenty-four of them. For when a Bey died the bravest of his followers was chosen to take his place. When the Mamelukes needed more men they either bought or stole children, very often from Europe, and brought them up as soldiers. They were trained to ride, shoot, and endure hardships while they were still very young. So they became the most splendid horsemen and marksmen, and fierce fighters. Mounted on fiery Arab steeds, armed with beautiful weapons, swords of finest steel, muskets and pistols inlaid with gold, dressed in rich and gorgeous robes, glittering with jewels, they dashed over the country, ruling and oppressing as they chose. Fierce and haughty, they made every one bow to their will. They considered all the wealth of the country as theirs, and they cruelly oppressed the poor Arabs, forcing them to work hard, and taking almost all their earnings from them.

It was against these Mamelukes that Napoleon now had to fight. He tried to make the Arabs and other peoples of Egypt join him, and help him to conquer their oppressors. But the poor Arabs, who hardly knew what right or freedom meant, only saw in him another conqueror, and were little willing to help him.

CHAPTER XIX

THE PYRAMIDS

It was July when Napoleon left Alexandria to march against the Mamelukes and take Cairo. Many of his soldiers were old and tried men. They had endured the heat of Italy cheerfully, for there, although the sun was hot, they had marched through fertile lands well watered and pleasant. At the end of the day's march food and wine were always to be had. But now, day by day they marched over burning sand, under a brazen sky, through a land barren and empty, where neither man nor beast was to be seen, and where there was scarce a growing thing but thorny shrubs.

With feet burned and blistered, with parched tongues and cracked lips, blinded by the glare of the sun upon the sand, maddened by swarms of flies and insects, the march became a torture to the men. Gasping in the intolerable heat, they threw off their clothes, trying to find relief. Was this where the general had promised them six acres of land? they angrily demanded.

Even the officers could hardly bear the fiery torment. They pulled off their cockades and trod them in the sand and murmured of rebellion. Napoleon alone seemed cool and calm. He wore his heavy uniform, buttoned up to the throat as usual, when the men were throwing away almost every garment. And when they were gasping and perspiring, he seemed as cool in body as in mind.

As the army wound along the weary way, many men, too worn out to keep up with the others, fell behind. Then out of the dust of the desert, through the glare of the dazzling sun, a company of fleet mounted Arabs would dash upon the stragglers. Then woe to them. Muskets cracked, bright steel flashed, and the blood of Frenchmen stained the yellow desert sand.

For a fortnight the toilsome march dragged on through the seemingly endless desert, until the men began to believe that there was no such place as Cairo. For the first time, they had lost faith in their leader. Then, at last, one day over the unbroken waste of desert there rose enormous masses in straight lines and angles. They were the Pyramids.

The Pyramids are the tombs of the ancient kings of Egypt, some of whom lived more than twenty-five hundred years B.C. They are enormous blocks of stone and brick, broad at the bottom and coming to a point at the top, many of them being higher than a high church tower. They are one of the wonders of the world, and after thousands of years they still stand, giant memorials of forgotten times.

Here, in this city of the dead, the Mamelukes awaited their enemy. Drawn out in glittering lines, with cannon pointed and camp entrenched, they waited.

Through a telescope Napoleon carefully examined the lines of the foe. He was a great general, but he noticed the smallest details. He now saw something which none of his officers had seen. The enemy's cannon were not on wheels. They were fixed, and could only be fired in one direction. That decided the day.

Napoleon drew up his men so that they should be out of range of the cannon. Then, pointing to the Pyramids as the battle began, "Soldiers," he cried, "forty centuries look down upon you."

And there in the sandy desert, under the burning sun, Mameluke and Frenchman fought. Flashing in the sunlight, the brilliant cavalcade came spurring on. Again and again it broke against the solid wall of glittering bayonets. The fight was fearful. When the Mamelukes could no longer shoot, they dashed their pistols in the faces of their enemies. When wounded, they crawled on the sand, hewing, hacking, and stabbing all that they could reach. But at last, scattered and thinned by the fearful charge of the French, the Mamelukes fled.

Battle of the pyramids

Many threw themselves into the Nile in the panic of flight. Many were cut down by the pursuing French. Those who escaped carried to all parts of Egypt the fame and terror of Sultan Kebir, the King of Fire, as they called Napoleon.

Four days after the battle of the Pyramids, Napoleon entered Cairo. Here, through its brilliant, narrow, dirty, ill-paved streets, ride, and walk, and jostle each other, men and women of every country and colour. The jabber of tongues, the shouts of donkey- and camel-drivers, the tinkle of bells, the cries of street merchants, all make up a perfect babel of sound, such as is only to be heard in Eastern cities.

And here for some months Napoleon made his headquarters, ruling and commanding, fighting and punishing, making new laws for Egypt, just as a few months before he had, after overturning all the kingdoms of Italy, formed them anew to please himself.

CHAPTER XX

NAPOLEON MARCHES INTO ASIA

But meanwhile Napoleon's conquests in Egypt had been made useless, for the French fleet had been destroyed. Soon after the French soldiers had been landed, Nelson at last found the enemy he had been seeking so long, although Napoleon had escaped him. When the French and British fleets met, the battle of the Nile was fought, in which the French were utterly defeated. Of that battle you will read in the Life of Nelson.

When the news of the battle was brought to Napoleon he was filled with grief. Not only had the British, whom he had hoped to crush, been victorious once more, but by that victory he and his soldiers were cut off from France. Then the Turks, no longer having the French fleet to fear, declared war with France, and made ready an army to attack Napoleon in Egypt.

This army was expected to land in Syria, and Napoleon decided to meet it there. So once more the weary march through burning desert began. With the French army, as before, went the learned men. They were treated with great respect, and rode upon asses. But the soldiers, as they trudged along through the burning sand, jeered at them. They had seen them wandering about the Pyramids, inspecting all the monuments and strange things of Egypt, and the soldiers had come to think that the whole expedition had been got up for them, and that they were the cause of all the misery. Yet when any danger arose they had to be protected. They were put in the middle, and the soldiers formed round them. "Make room for the asses!" they would cry; "make room for the asses!"

In those days there was no Suez Canal, and the army marched out of Africa into Asia across the isthmus. But although there was no canal when Napoleon marched across the isthmus, there had been one in olden times, and Napoleon actually gave orders that a new canal should be begun.

Nothing came of it, however, and it was left to another Frenchman, called Ferdinand de Lesseps, to plan and carry out the great work much later. This canal was begun in 1859 and opened ten years after, having cost nineteen millions to build. It is about a hundred miles long, and it makes the journey to India about three thousand miles shorter than by the old way round the Cape of Good Hope, and it has been of immense service in the trade of the world.

After crossing the isthmus, Napoleon took the fortress of El-Arish. Here the garrison were allowed to go free, after promising never again to fight against the French. He next took Gaza, the famous city of the Philistines, from which Samson carried away the gates, and where his grave is still pointed out. The army then marched to Jaffa.

Jaffa has now a very poor harbour, but in the days of Solomon it was the port for Jerusalem. In times much later it played a great part in the Crusades, and was captured from the Saracens by Richard Cœur de Lion. Now it is a little town with dirty, narrow streets, but it is surrounded by orange groves, of which fruit it exports great quantities, as well as of other fruits, grain, and wool, and is once more growing in importance.

When Napoleon reached Jaffa it had strong walls around it, and it was some days before he could make a breach in them. But at last the town was taken by storm. Then the French soldiers rushed in and began a horrible slaughter of the Turks. This at last was stopped by some of Napoleon's officers, and about three thousand wretched men were saved and made prisoners.

"What do you want me to do with them?" cried Napoleon in

anger when he saw the crowd of prisoners. "Have I food to feed them or ships in which to carry them away

"You told us to stop the slaughter," pleaded the officers.

"Yes, of women, and children, and old men, but not of soldiers," replied Napoleon, still more angry.

It was true: there was not enough food for every one. The French soldiers themselves had hardly enough to eat, and it made them angry to have to give some of their scanty fare to prisoners.

There was only one thing to do, and that was to let the men go free after promising that they would not again fight. But that Napoleon would not do.

"They will fight against us again, whatever they promise," he said. "They have done so already. These are the very men who were set free at El-Arish."

Then Napoleon gave an order which is one of the blackest things against his memory. "Let them be shot," he said.

So the wretched prisoners were led out of the town to the sandy shore, and there, to a man, they were shot and bayoneted in cold blood. They did not try to escape. They met death with the hopeless courage of the Eastern. It was fate.

CHAPTER XXI

THE RETURN FROM EGYPT

After the horrible slaughter of Jaffa, the French marched on to Acre. We remember this town chiefly as a town famous in the time of the Crusades. It was called St. Jean d'Acre, from the Knights of St. John who settled here. It was the port by which the Crusaders generally landed. Among these was Richard Coeur de Lion, who took the town from the Saracens.

In the time of Napoleon there was a cruel ruler who lived there, called Jessar Pasha, "the Butcher." Napoleon sent a message to this chief, hoping to win him to his side. But the Butcher cut off the messenger's head and threw his body into the sea in a sack.

So Napoleon began to besiege Acre. But now he had more than Turks against him. For Sir Sidney Smith, a British captain, was anchored in the bay, with two British ships, and he helped the Turks with men and guns.

For two months the siege went on. Napoleon had no bat-tering-guns with which to break down the walls, for Sir Sidney Smith had seized his ships as they were coming from Alexandria with them. So he could make little impression. Then the plague broke out among his men, and at last, sorely against his will, Napoleon was forced to give up the siege and march back. In the darkness and silence of a May night the French army crept away. Thus ended Napoleon's dreams of power in the East. He had been beaten by the one enemy who was always to beat him-the British. For had no British ships been in the bay of Acre, the town might have fallen. "Had St. Jean d'Acre fallen, I would have changed the face of the world," said Napoleon.

The retreat from Acre was one long agony. The sun blazed down upon the weary and now disheartened soldiers, many of whom were wounded and ill. Those who were too ill to walk were carried in litters. But sometimes the men, tired of carrying their wounded comrades, and themselves scarcely able to drag along, would throw them down, and leave them to die by the wayside or fall into the hands of the terrible Turks.

Sometimes the thirsting troops would see a cool oasis, with waving palm-trees and glimmering water-pools, in the distance. Eagerly they would press forward, only to find, a few moments later, that what they had seen was a mirage, a deceitful picture of the desert.

Sometimes, when they did find water, it was so foul or salty that their thirst was made worse rather than better. And all the way they were beset by pursuing Turks and wild desert Arabs, so that many more died on the march than in the battle. But at last their miseries were ended, and the worn-out army reached Cairo again.

Here Napoleon set himself once more to the ruling of Egypt, and by a great victory over the Turks at Aboukir Bay he blotted out the memory of his defeat at Acre.

All during the time of the Syrian campaign Napoleon had had no news of France. Now some old newspapers came into his hands. From them he learned that things were indeed going ill at home. Italy was lost, and all his great conquests were wiped out as if they had never been.

"The fools have lost Italy," he exclaimed. "All the fruits of my victories have disappeared. I must leave Egypt."

But he had no ships in which to carry his army home. So he resolved to go alone, taking only about five hundred men with him, and leaving one of his generals in charge of the campaign, which from the beginning had been utterly useless.

Napoleon made all his preparations with great secrecy. He

dare not tell his soldiers that he was going to desert them. One dark August night, under the pale light of the twinkling stars, as silently as possible, the company rode down to the harbour of Alexandria. Quickly and stealthily the men went on board two waiting vessels. The horses could not be taken, so they were turned loose. They, left riderless and free, turned by instinct and galloped back to Alexandria. There the people, awaking in fear at the sound of horses galloping wildly through the streets, thought it was some new invasion, until it was discovered that the horses belonged to the French army.

In spite of some victories, the Egyptian campaign had been an utter failure. For a year of fighting, suffering, and misery, there was no gain to show. There was, on the other hand, the loss of a fleet of ships, of more than six thousand soldiers, besides many guns and cannon.

But when Napoleon returned to France, the people greeted him more joyfully than ever. They were weary of the rule of the Directory, and longed for a change. Napoleon had never meant to be a soldier and conqueror only; he meant to be a ruler too. He now saw his chance and took it.

CHAPTER XXII

FIRST CONSUL OF FRANCE

Soon after Napoleon returned from Egypt he was made commander of all the troops round Paris. Then one day he appeared at the head of his soldiers in the courtyard of the palace in which the French Assembly, or Parliament, sat. Amid a fearful noise of shouts, beating of drums, and tramp of feet the Assembly was turned out at the point of the bayonet. That night Napoleon slept in the palace of the Luxembourg, with the title of Consul of France.

There were three other consuls. But that was a mere pretence. Napoleon was the true ruler. One morning on the walls of Paris a placard appeared like this:-

POLITICAL SUBTRACTION
From 5 Directors
take 2
There remains 3 Consuls
From them take
2 Consuls
and there remains 1 Bonaparte.

So you see that already people knew that Napoleon was master.

It was October when Napoleon returned from Egypt. By the middle of December he was First Consul, and for the next few months he gave himself up to ruling. Under his firm hand France, which had been torn and tossed in wild unrest for eight years, now seemed to find a little calm.

But all around the borders of France there was war still. Austria and Britain were her chief enemies. With Britain, at this time, Napoleon would have been glad to make peace, could he have done so on his own terms. Austria he meant to crush, and to crush in such a way as would make Europe ring with the name of Bonaparte. He meant to do great deeds at which the world would stare and wonder. He meant to have peace too, but peace after victory.

The army of Italy was still fighting under a brave general called Massena. But now he was shut up in Genoa, a British fleet bombarding him from the sea, and an Austrian army surrounding him on land. Food was growing scarce, and his men were but worn-out skeletons. The Austrians believed that they should very soon beat him, and then they would be able to march into France. On the Rhine was another army under a leader called Moreau, whose fame was scarcely less than Napoleon's.

Napoleon now gathered a third army, called the Reserve, with which, he gave out, he was going to march to the help of Massena. But the Austrians laughed at the Reserve army, for it was made up of ill-fed, half-clothed, raw recruits. Napoleon went to Dijon to review these new recruits. But he stayed there only two hours and was soon speeding on his way to Geneva.

For three months Napoleon had been silently and secretly gathering troops which by different ways had been sent towards Switzerland. There, too, engineers had been sent to examine the passes through the Alps. Now everything was ready, and the great commander also went speeding to the land of snow mountains.

Switzerland is the only country in Europe which has no sea-coast whatever. On every side it is surrounded by other lands. Yet in the struggle and wars of nations Switzerland has suffered less than some. There are few battlefields here, and for hundreds of years the name of Switzerland has stood for freedom. High mountains form a great part of the boundaries of Switzerland, and the country itself is full of mountains, there being little flat land. This would make it hard to conquer.

Many of these mountains are so high that snow lies upon them all the year round. For the higher you rise in the air the colder it becomes. Just as the further north you travel the colder it becomes, until near the pole snow lies all the year round. Thus on a Swiss mountainside you can pass through several climates.

In the low valleys and slopes are found rich fields where abundant crops of corn and vines, tobacco and fruits, grow as in the plains of sunny France, and where figs and almonds will ripen in the open air. Higher up on the mountain slopes are the meadows, where sheep and cattle graze, and where dairy-farming and cheese-making are carried on in summer. For in winter both flocks and shepherds come down to the valleys to shelter from the fierce cold and snows until the spring returns. Higher still are wild regions where no one lives even in summer, and where only the chamois is hunted. And above that again is the region of perpetual snow, where scarcely any animal can live, and only the most hardy alpine plants can grow.

One reason why Switzerland has not been fought over so much as some other lands is that it would not be a great prize when it was conquered.

Although the country is beautiful the land is not very fertile. More than a quarter of it is glaciers and stone, or is in other ways quite useless, either as agricultural or pastoral land. It has also no mineral wealth. Its wealth lies in the hardy, thrifty, industrious character of its people. Therefore, although it has no sea-coast, canals, or navigable rivers, which fact makes commerce difficult, and although it has no coal, which makes manufacturing difficult, it has become a manufacturing country. The energies of the people have adapted the conditions of their country to their needs. Thus, the place of coal is supplied by the plentiful water-power of countless streams which come from the mountainsides. These streams are always full, for the high mountains catch the rain-clouds in winter, and in summer the sun melts the eternal snows which lie upon their summits.

And to such good purpose do the Swiss use this water-power that many Swiss villages are lit with electric light, while villages of the same size in this country would be lit by oil-lamps, or at best by gas.

The manufactures are those which require either little raw material, or which are made of the raw material supplied by the country itself. Thus, much of Switzerland being covered with forest, a great industry in wood-carving, wooden clocks, and musical boxes has grown up. Great quantities of cheese and condensed milk are made upon the alpine pastures. Woollen cloths are made from the wool of the sheep and goats.

Of the manufactures which require imported material watch-making is one of the chief. This does not require much or heavy material, as the value of the article, when finished, lies greatly in the skill of the workmen. Many Swiss towns, too, manufacture silk, the raw material for which can easily be brought from Italy and France, where it is grown. This is especially so since the boring of tunnels through the Alps. Embroidery, on muslin and linen, is another great Swiss industry.

But the beauty of the country is perhaps what adds most to its wealth. For each year thousands of people go there from every country of Europe. In the winter, they go for skating and tobogganing, in the spring and autumn, to sail upon the lakes and climb the mountains, until, as every geography book will tell you, it has become the playground of Europe.

Geneva, to which Napoleon now went, is one of the largest towns in Switzerland. It is the chief seat of the watch factories, and besides being in a very beautiful situation, it is interesting in many ways. It was here that Rousseau was born. Calvin lived here, and John Knox, too, for a short time.

When Napoleon arrived he gathered his engineers around him and began to study the map of the Alps.

"Is it possible to pass?" he asked.

"It is barely possible," said an engineer.

"Very well," replied Napoleon; "let us be going."

CHAPTER XXIII

NAPOLEON CROSSES THE ALPS

Napoleon now began one of his most famous marches. Once before he had passed the Alps by rounding them. This time he meant to cross them, and, while the enemy awaited him in front, appear suddenly behind.

The army was divided into four, each part going by a different way. The paths through the mountains are called passes. The passes which Napoleon now chose were the Great St. Bernard, the Little St. Bernard, the Mont Cenis, and the St. Gothard. Napoleon himself went by the Great St. Bernard.

It was a tremendous march which now began, for in places there was not even a track, and the men had to stumble as best they could over rough, broken, stony ground. Up and up they struggled, for a pass is only comparatively low; that is, low when compared with the huge mountains near. The Great St. Bernard pass is more than eight thousand feet above sea-level. It was hard enough for men laden with knapsack and gun to toil upwards, but to drag heavy cannon up was still harder. The path was so terrible that it was found to be quite impossible to bring them up on their carriages. No wheels could pass over the ground, so each cannon was taken from its carriage, and was put into the trunk of a tree, which had been hollowed out to fit it. A hundred men were then harnessed to each tree-trunk, and so the cannon were dragged over snow and ice, along narrow, giddy paths where only the chamois or the goatherd had left a path. The carriages were taken to pieces, the wheels were slung on poles and carried on men's shoulders.

Food for the army had to be carried too. This was laden on mules. They were sure-footed, hardy beasts, accustomed to the wild mountainsides, and so could carry weight even over the rough path. But with the cavalry horses it was different. The men dismounted, and each man led his horse as best he could.

Thus for five days an endless stream of men and horses passed among the silent hills, churning the white snow into a brown morass, filling the still air with the hum of voices, and the clank and jingle of steel, awaking the echoes with the sound of drum and trumpet. On and on went the men, slipping, sliding, panting, breathless, hardly daring to pause in places lest those behind should be thrown into confusion, stumbling knee-deep into snowdrifts, clambering round boulders, but always upward and upward. At last they reached the summit of the pass.

Here is the Hospice of St. Bernard, founded by St. Bernard de Menthon nearly a thousand years ago. And here all the year round live the good monks of St. Bernard, ever ready to aid travellers, and seek for those who may be lost among the mountains. In this they are helped by the famous St. Bernard dogs, whose sense of smell is so strong that they can find travellers, even when they lie buried in the snow.

Here it is so high, and therefore so cold, that the winter lasts nine months. Only in July, August, and September does the snow melt. And even then the little lake beside the Hospice is sometimes frozen over during the night. When the wearied soldiers reached the top of the pass the good monks gave them a meal of bread and wine and cheese, and then the long descent began. For the horses and mules this was almost more difficult than the ascent. But sliding and stumbling they at last got over the worst of the road with no serious accident.

But a new difficulty now arose. Fort Bard had to be passed. This was only a little fort held by four hundred Austrians, but, perched upon a rock, it commanded the tiny town through which the road lay, and the whole pass, which here is not more than fifty yards wide.

For some time the French tried in vain to take the fort. Then at length they discovered a narrow goat-track leading round it, and out of gun-shot. By this, one by one, the infantry passed, but it was impossible to take the artillery that way. So in the dead of night the artillery-men entered the village. They spread chaff and straw upon the street, and having muffled every belt or buckle that might clatter or jingle, they drew the cannon through the town, almost under the noses of the unsuspecting Austrians.

Then, the last difficulty being passed, the French poured like an avalanche down upon the plain of Italy.

The news of Napoleon's wonderful march soon reached the famished garrison of Genoa, and the thought that help was near renewed their sinking courage. But day after day passed, and no rescuing French army appeared before the walls. Still they hoped on, sick at heart and weary. But at length the last spark of hope died, and brave Massena gave in. They had absolutely nothing left to eat but knapsacks and shoes, grass and roots.

"No terms are too good for you," said Lord Keith, the British commander. So the French were allowed to march out with all the honours of war.

CHAPTER XXIV

THE WORLD AT PEACE

Meanwhile Napoleon was marching on Milan, passing through Italy in a kind of triumph. It did not suit his plans to relieve Genoa, so he left the garrison to starve, while he prepared for a great battle in which all was to be won or lost.

And so at last French and Austrian met again upon the field of Marengo, a little village not far from the town of Alessandria.

At daybreak on the 14th of June the fight began. It was a fierce and terrible battle. The Austrians numbered nearly twice as many as the French. At one time the French fled from the field, crying "All is lost." Again they rallied, but step by step they were driven backward, and at last fled once more. The Austrian leader was an old man of over eighty. He was weary of long fighting, and about three o'clock in the afternoon, believing the victory won, he left the field.

But at this moment a French officer who had been at some distance rode up, with fresh troops. "I fear it is a battle lost," he said to Napoleon.

"I think it is a battle won," replied he. And rallying his men, and ordering a sudden charge of cavalry, he turned defeat into victory. Soon it was the Austrians who were fleeing from the field in utter rout.

So completely crushed was the Austrian army that next day their leader sent a flag of truce to Napoleon, begging for peace. And by the treaty which followed all Northern Italy was given up, almost as it had been at the treaty of Campo-Formio. Thus at one blow was Italy reconquered.

Having thus startled the world, and covered his name with glory, Napoleon returned to Paris. He had been gone less than two months. All along the way people crowded to cheer him as he passed. In Paris the houses were lit up night after night in his honour. For hours together crowds would stand round his palace hoping to catch a glimpse of the conqueror of the Alps, of the victor of Marengo. Napoleon was delighted with all the fame he had won. "A few more events like this campaign, and I shall perhaps go down to posterity," he cried.

France now made peace with all Europe. But it was not until many months later that peace was made with Britain. First, Napoleon persuaded many of the powers of Europe to join together against Britain in what was called an Armed Neutrality. But Nelson put an end to that by winning the Battle of the Baltic. Next, Sir Ralph Abercrombie and Lord Keith beat the French in Egypt, and at last drove them out of that country again. By this time both the French and British people wanted peace, so on the 25th of March 1802, after fifteen years or more of war, peace was signed. This was called the Peace of Amiens.

Among other things in this treaty, Britain received the islands of Ceylon and Trinidad, and agreed to give back the island of Malta to the Knights of St. John.

Meanwhile Napoleon was busy ruling France, and these few years are really the best part of all his life. In them he did many good things for France. And these lasted when all his great conquests faded, and his vast Empire crumbled into pieces.

Ever since the Revolution, France had been tossed about from one form of government to another. Now again the country had a safe and steady government.

At the Revolution the French had done away with all religion. With that had gone Sunday, and the week was made to have ten days instead of seven. Napoleon had fought against the Pope and had taken his lands away from him. Now he made friends with the Pope, and brought back the Roman Catholic religion to France once more. He did not do this because he cared about such things, but because he thought that it was wise. He had tried to make friends with the people of Egypt, who were Mussulmans, by telling them that he too was a Mussulman, and that he had overthrown the Pope, but now when it suited him he made friends with him.

A new university was now opened. The Bank of France was founded, new laws were passed. These new laws which were made in the time of Napoleon, and which received the name of the Code of Napoleon, are the laws by which France is still ruled.

It was now, too, that Napoleon founded the Legion of Honour. This was an honour given to any one who had done anything worthy of reward. It was given to soldiers or civilians alike. And to this day it is considered perhaps the greatest honour a Frenchman may win.

At the Revolution even the names of the months and the number of the years had been changed. The 22nd of September was New Year's Day, and 1792 was year 1. The months were called by names which were supposed to explain them. January was called Rainymonth, February, Windymonth, and so on. In writing letters to people in other countries, who counted the days and years in the old way, this was very awkward. Indeed it must have been very awkward for the French themselves, and very difficult to remember. So, soon after this the French people gave it up, and went back to the old way.

In fact in every way they became more like other people again. Men and women were no longer called citizen and citizeness, but Madame and Monsieur. Many of the nobles who had fled returned to their homes. They brought back with them the grand manners of the time of Louis, and by degrees the drawing-room of the First Consul began to look like the court of a king.

"You see everything returns," said Napoleon to an old and stern republican.

"Yes," he replied bitterly, "everything returns—everything except the two millions of Frenchmen who died to destroy what you are building up again."

Before the Revolution France had been divided into provinces.

Each province had its own customs, and sometimes even a language of its own. To do away with this, France was at the Revolution divided into eighty-seven departments. These departments were all made as much as possible the same size, and were called after the chief rivers or mountains which they enclosed. This has never been changed, and France is still divided into departments, although the old names of the provinces are still used too.

CHAPTER XXV

NAPOLEON CONSUL FOR LIFE

Gradually Napoleon's power grew greater and greater. But still he had only been made Consul for ten years. The Senate now proposed that the time should be increased to twenty years. But that did not please Napoleon. So he thanked them, and said that he could not rule longer than ten years, unless it was the will of the people. The voice of the people must be heard first, he said.

So the people were asked. But the question which they were asked was not "Shall Napoleon be Consul for twenty years?" but "Shall Napoleon be Consul for life?"

All over the country books were sent, in which people could write their names, and say "Yes" or "No" in answer to this question. Only a few hundred said "No," although many did not vote at all, and so Napoleon was proclaimed Consul for life on the 15th of August 1802.

But this time of peace for France and for Europe did not last long. By the peace of Amiens, you remember, Malta was to be given back to the Knights of St. John. But the British were very slow to do this. They feared that if they did, the island would very soon fall again into the hands of Napoleon. For he was doing many things on the Continent which showed that he wished to gain for France more power than was safe for the peace and liberty of the rest of Europe.

Among other things, he made himself Grand Mediator or Overlord of Switzerland. The very name of Switzerland has since the days of Tell stood for liberty. It made every country in Europe angry that Napoleon should so try to crush the old spirit of freedom. Yet Britain alone sent a messenger to protest against such oppression and greed. But Napoleon would not listen. "These are only trifles," he said. However, as long as he did such things Britain resolved to keep Malta. But Napoleon was determined that Malta should be given up. "I would rather see the British in the suburbs of Paris," he said, "than in Malta."

Both countries, at this time, hated and were jealous of each other. Both knew that the peace of Amiens was not truly a peace, but only a truce. Napoleon tried his best to ruin British trade. And on 16th May 1803, little more than a year after the signing of the peace, war was once more declared by Britain.

Napoleon made believe to be very angry when war was declared. Perhaps he was angry, for although he hoped one day to crush Britain, he was not yet ready. Many of his soldiers had gone on leave after their hard years of fighting. Most of the cannon had been sent to the foundries to be recast, and in many ways he was unprepared.

But with Napoleon a difficulty only brought out his quickness and genius. Soon men were everywhere gathering and drilling. Soon every port was noisy with shipbuilding, and hundreds of flat-bottomed boats were got ready to carry a great army over the sea to invade Britain. Harbours were enlarged to make room for this new fleet, all France indeed was busy with preparation.

Napoleon himself visited the ports and harbours to see how the works were going on. Then he made a tour through Belgium.

Belgium is a very small country, and has very little coast-line, only forty miles in all. And the whole of that forty miles is a long, low, almost unbroken, sandy shore. The sea is kept from flowing over the land either by natural sand-banks or by stone walls. Along this shore Ostend is the only port, and it is chiefly a passenger port, Ostend itself being a fashionable seaside town, where every year thousands of people go for holidays.

The great port of Belgium, to which Napoleon now went,

is Antwerp on the Scheld. It is not only the greatest seaport in Belgium but one of the finest in the world. It is also one of the strongest fortresses, and is the chief arsenal of the kingdom. It is thought that an army of two hundred and fifty thousand would be required to besiege it, and that even then it could hold out for a year.

Belgium has need of very strong fortresses, as it has no natural barriers to keep enemies out in time of war. Neither high mountains, nor wide rivers, guard its borders. It lies, too, surrounded by other lands—France, Germany, and Holland, and for this reason it has often become the battlefield of other nations in quarrels not its own.

But the same causes which make Belgium easy to invade make trade with it easy. So Antwerp has become an outlet for German as well as for Belgian commerce. It is also the most convenient port by which British goods can reach central Europe.

Antwerp has manufactures too, for it can easily get coal from the coalfield which stretches along the valley of the Meuse and the Sambre, from Liege to Charleroi, and from there on to the borders of France. This coalfield is really the same as the French coalfield of Valenciennes

Antwerp has also long been famous for its diamond-cutting industry. And besides all this trade, Antwerp is one of the most interesting towns of Europe. Its narrow streets are full of quaint old houses and beautiful churches, the chief of which is the Cathedral, with its splendid spire. Its galleries are full of beautiful pictures, and some of the most famous Flemish artists lived and worked here, of whom perhaps Rubens, Van Dyke, and Teniers are the best known.

But when Napoleon visited Antwerp it was not the great port that it is now. He was quick to see, however, what a strong position the town held, and he at once gave orders for the building and improving of docks and harbour.

CHAPTER XXVI

MORE BELGIAN TOWNS

From Antwerp Napoleon went to Brussels. Brussels is now the capital of Belgium and has been called the "little Paris," so full is it of beautiful streets and buildings. Besides being the capital, it has also breweries, leather-works, and other important manufactures, and is famous for its lace.

Most of Belgium is quite flat. The only hills are in the Ardennes in the south-east, and they are not very high. Here there is much good pasture-land where sheep, cattle, and horses are bred. Flanders horses have long been famous. You remember, perhaps, that Henry VIII. Rudely called his wife, Anne of Cleves, a Flanders mare. The soil of Belgium is very sandy by nature, but the people have tilled it so carefully that now it has become in many places very fertile. Much flax is grown, from which the famous Brussels lace is made, and which supplies the linen-mills of Ypres.

Having a great coalfield and also good iron ore, Belgium is really a mining and manufacturing country, more than an agricultural one. In the valley of the Meuse from Liege to Namur, among the ruined castles of days gone by, rise tall factory chimneys, and the flames from iron-furnaces light up the sky, and the clatter and clang of machinery sounds all day long.

Of this district, Liege is the centre. Here are gun-factories and cannon-foundries, engine, machinery, and cycle works. Liege fire-arms are famous all the Continent over. In the suburb Seraing is the famous Cotterill ironworks, founded about a hundred years ago by an Englishman, John Cotterill. Here the first locomotive made on the Continent was built.

There is an old Latin verse which says, "Brussels rejoiced in noble men, Antwerp in money, Ghent in halters, Bruges in pretty girls, Louvain in learned men, and Malines in fools." Malines, however, whether famous for fools or not, gave its name to a beautiful kind of lace, but very little is made there now. And Bruges, once one of the centres of the world's trade, seems to have stood still for several centuries, so that, wandering along its narrow, crooked streets, and by its many canals, one can easily picture what it looked like many many years ago.

Ghent is said to be famous for halters, because in olden times the people of Ghent were often unruly, and once, having rebelled against their lord, they were made to appear before him with halters round their necks, as a sign of submission. Now the city is famous for its nursery gardens. It exports whole cargoes of flowers, being indeed called "the town of flowers." For although it is not a seaport it is connected with the Scheld, and so with the sea, by a ship canal. It has also cotton and linen factories, and exports coal, wood, flax, etc.

But to us, one of the most interesting things about Ghent is that there, in 1340, John of Gaunt, the son of Edward I., was born, and from that received his name.

Napoleon visited all these busy towns, taking great interest in the manufactures, and asking questions about all he saw. Then he returned to Paris, visiting Rheims on the way.

Round Rheims the hills are planted with vineyards, and it is one of the chief centres for the wine trade of Champagne. It is also one of the great centres of the woollen trade, and manufactures a special kind of cloth, a mixture of silk and wool.

But Rheims is chiefly interesting and famous as the crowning-place of the kings of France. There, in the grand cathedral, the kings of France had been crowned and anointed ever since the twelfth century. Napoleon, as he stood beneath the splendid dome, was full of secret longings and desires. He knew himself to be one of the greatest rulers that France had ever had. But he was still uncrowned. He was neither king nor emperor, but only Consul.

CHAPTER XXVII

THE EMPEROR

Napoleon, like all stern rulers, had enemies. There were many people in France who hated him, and who, in spite of all they had suffered under the Bourbons, longed to have a king again. So there were plots to kill Napoleon and to put the brother of Louis XVI. on the throne.

About this time one of these plots was discovered and, rightly or wrongly, many people were put to death; others were imprisoned, others banished from the land.

Among those who were put to death was the Duke d'Enghien, one of the greatest nobles of France. Nothing was ever proved against him, and after a mere mockery of a trial, in the dead of night, he was led out into the courtyard of the castle of Vincennes, and shot at six o'clock one grey March morning.

All the princes of Europe were filled with horror at this murder, for it was little else. But they did nothing to avenge it, and then the friends of Napoleon used the plot to gain what he had long wanted. That was to make him king in name as well as in deed. They said that he must make his rule so sure, that not only should he govern during his life, but his children after him should rule. They said that people were less likely to try to kill Napoleon if they knew that after his death he would be succeeded by a Bonaparte, and that there was no hope that a Bourbon should ever again sit upon the throne.

"At sight of the danger from which our hero has been saved," they said, "we cannot but think that those who wished to destroy the Consul strove to destroy France. Great Man! finish your work, and make it immortal as your glory. You have brought us out of the confusion of the past; you help us to enjoy the blessings of the present; make us also sure of the future."

So, with many grand speeches and much flattery, Napoleon was asked to become Emperor. He took that title rather than king, because he thought it would please the soldiers better. Besides, it reminded people of the great Emperor Charlemagne, whose kingdom had stretched far over other lands, and whose greatness Napoleon wished to equal or surpass.

On the 18th of May 1804 he was proclaimed Emperor of the French.

The "little corporal" had come far. He who, a few years before, had wandered almost penniless among the streets of Paris, was now the greatest man in all the land. He seemed to have reached the very highest power that man could hope for, and he was not yet thirty-five years old.

No sooner did Napoleon become Emperor than he made all his brothers and sisters princes and princesses, and gave titles to many of his friends. Clad in splendid robes, and surrounded by a glittering company of officers, the Emperor and Empress drove through the streets amid the cheers of the people, and especially of the soldiers.

Now truly the French Republic was at an end. The people no longer ruled. The army was the greatest power in the land, and Napoleon was both the master and the darling of the army.

Every ruler in Europe, except the Kings of Great Britain, and of Sweden, and the Czar of Russia, sent messages to the new Emperor, wishing him good fortune. Some of the lesser German princes even came themselves to Paris, so great was his power over all Europe.

Soon after he was proclaimed Emperor, Napoleon went to Boulogne to review the army, which was still making ready to invade Britain.

Boulogne is the chief station in France of the North Sea fisheries. It is a port, and does a good deal of trade, but it is chiefly a mail and passenger packet station between Britain and France. But it imports a good deal of raw material and has manufacturies of cloth and leather.

When Napoleon arrived here he was received with cheers even louder than those which had greeted him as he drove through the streets of Paris. There were grand ceremonies, and much speech-making. At the review which he held, Napoleon gave the Cross of the Legion of Honour to many old soldiers who had fought with him in Egypt and in Italy. Napoleon loved to act a part. He loved to please and astonish people both in great and little things. So he would say to his officers, "Find out what men have fought in Egypt or in Italy, and tell me their names and numbers." Then as he walked down the lines, if he saw a man whose number he had been told of, he would go up to him and say, "Ah, so you are here. You are a brave fellow. I remember you at Aboukir. How is your old father? What, you have no medal! See! I will give you the Cross."

And the men, quite deceived by this little piece of acting, would say to each other, "See, the Emperor knows us all. He remembers our names, and even knows about our families." So they became more willing than ever to fight and die for such a commander.

There is another story told of Napoleon about this time which is much pleasanter to remember.

Two British sailors who had been kept prisoner in France managed to escape. They reached Boulogne, and there remained in hiding for some time, living as best they could, for they had no money, and how to cross the sea they did not know. But at last they succeeded in getting together some small pieces of wood and a bit of sail-cloth. Out of this they made a tiny boat. It was only about four feet wide, and very little longer. But in this tiny cockleshell they made up their minds to set sail, and try to reach home. It was better to be drowned than to be shot, they thought; and they certainly would be shot if they were discovered.

So one day, seeing a British ship not far out to sea, they launched their little skiff, hoping to get near enough to be picked up by her. But they had only gone a very short way when they were seen and brought back by the French.

The story of these two daring men went through the camp, and at last even Napoleon heard of them. He always loved brave deeds, so he ordered the men and their boat to be brought before him. When they appeared, he looked at them in surprise and admiration.

"Is it true," he asked, "that you thought of crossing the sea in this tiny boat?"

"Sire," they answered, "if you doubt it, give us leave to go, and you shall soon see."

"I do give you leave," replied Napoleon; "but you shall not risk your lives. You are free. And when you get back to London, tell them there that I love brave men, even if they are my enemies."

The Emperor then gave them some money and sent them on board a ship going to England.

CHAPTER XXVIII

THE CROWNING OF THE EMPEROR

Although Napoleon had been proclaimed Emperor, and accepted by the people of France, he had not yet been crowned. Now he felt that to be crowned and anointed by the Pope would make his throne more sure. So he sent a friend to Rome, to ask the Pope to come to crown him.

Pope Pius VII. did not want to crown Napoleon, and acknowledge him as the rightful ruler of France. But he saw that nearly all the other rulers of Europe had acknowledged him, so he thought it better to do so too, as perhaps he might in that way win something good for the Church. He consented, therefore, to come to Paris to crown the Emperor.

The Pope, as head of the Church, had been treated with fear and reverence by the proudest of kings in all ages and in all countries. They had knelt to him as to one greater than themselves. But Napoleon had grown so proud that he could not bear the thought of kneeling to any one. So, although he very well knew the hour at which the Pope might be expected to arrive, he arranged to meet him as if by accident while out hunting.

As the Pope's coach drove along the road leading to the palace of Fontainebleau, which had been prepared for him, he met the Emperor, booted and spurred, and riding upon a horse.

The Emperor got off his horse, and the Pope, in his beautiful robes and white silk shoes, left his coach, and walked a few steps along the muddy road to greet him.

The young Emperor and the old Pope embraced each other, then the servants, having received their orders before, drove the coach up between them. The footmen opened both doors at once, and as the Pope stepped in at one side the Emperor stepped in at the other, so neither went in before the other. But Napoleon took care that he had the seat of honour, on the right side. Thus Pope and Emperor drove to Fontainebleau.

There were a great many preparations for the coronation to be made, for Napoleon meant it to be a very fine affair. But at last everything was ready, and on the 2nd of December the coronation took place. The day was cold and bleak, but the streets of Paris were lined with people, eager to see the Emperor and Empress as they drove in their gilded carriage to the Church of Notre Dame.

The church was thronged with fair ladies and splendid men glittering with jewels and lace, and as the Emperor entered, wearing upon his head a wreath of golden bay-leaves like a Caesar, the archways of the dim old church rang and rang again with shouts, "Long live the Emperor! Long live the Emperor!"

The notes of the organ rolled, the voices of the choir rose and fell in chant and hymn. But as the long ceremony went on, Napoleon yawned and fidgeted. To him there was nothing sacred or solemn in the service. The grand display added something to his pomp and glory; that was all.

At last the Pope with trembling hands lifted the crown to place it upon the young Emperor's head. But Napoleon, seizing it out of the Pope's hand, himself placed it upon his own head, took it off, placed it for a moment on the head of the Empress, and then returned it to the cushion upon which it had rested. Again the organ pealed, and the exultant words of the "Te Deum" rang out through the church.

The Emperor was crowned.

A few months after the coronation at Notre Dame, Napoleon went to Italy. Here, in the great cathedral at Milan, he again crowned himself. This time the title he took was King of Italy, and this time the Pope sternly refused to have anything to do with

Napoleon and the Pope

it. At Paris he had received only empty promises and insults as his reward, and he now knew that he had nothing to hope from the new Emperor.

At Notre Dame Napoleon had been crowned with the crown of Charlemagne. At Milan it was the ancient iron crown of Lombardy that he placed upon his head. This crown of Lombardy is a plain circle of iron, covered with gold. The iron circle is said to have been made from the nails of the Cross.

As Napoleon placed this ancient crown upon his head he cried aloud, "God has given it to me. Let him who touches it beware."

The great musician Beethoven was living at this time. He was a republican, and he admired Napoleon very much, believing him to be a true republican, and he dedicated one of his most beautiful pieces of music to him—"From Beethoven to Bonaparte," he wrote upon it simply. Now, when he heard that Napoleon had made himself an Emperor and a King, he tore off the dedication in wrath, cursing him as a tyrant. Many years later he sadly dedicated the music again to Napoleon, but this time he wrote upon it-

"To the memory of a great man."

CHAPTER XXIX

ABOUT THE GERMAN EMPIRE

It was now two years since war between France and Britain had been declared. Yet the French had done nothing except make great preparations.

The British, too, had made great preparations. Volunteers flocked in from every side. Every man who could hold a gun was eager to help to defend his country. Soon, besides the regular soldiers, there were three hundred and fifty thousand men in arms. Everywhere along the coast beacons were built and watches were set. On every hill-top bonfires were laid ready, so that should the dreadful "Bonny," as he was called, land, the news could be flashed from peak to peak, to warn men to rally to the defence of their homes. Night and day the watch was kept, but the "Ogre of Corsica," of whom such dreadful tales were told that women and children trembled at his name, never arrived.

The British fleet scoured the seas, watching the ports of France, guarding the shores of Britain. In vain the French admiral tried to decoy the British ships away. For it was Napoleon's great plan to decoy the British far away on some false scent. Then, protected by French warships, his great navy of flat-bottomed boats would sail across the Channel, and a hundred thousand men would be poured upon the English shore before the British fleet could return to stop them.

But the British admirals were too wary. The time never came when the weather was calm enough, and the British far enough away, to make the crossing safe. So the great army of England remained in camp at Boulogne, drilling and manoeuvring, and helping to build harbours, and cut canals, while waiting until the time should come for them to conquer Britain.

But while Napoleon was placing crowns upon his own head, the rulers of Europe were again joining against him. For they saw that the Emperor's power, and desire for still more power, were becoming so great that none of their crowns were safe.

Sweden, Russia, and Austria joined the alliance. But, on the other hand, Spain and Britain having quarrelled, Spain joined with France against the others. Once more Europe was ablaze with war. Upon the Rhine, in Tyrol, and in Italy, there was noise of battle. Napoleon gave up the idea of invading Britain in the meantime. The army of England was marched away from the camp at Boulogne to the borders of Germany. The Czar of Russia gathered a great army and sent it to join the Austrians. When they joined, it was intended that both armies should march together into France.

But the Austrians began to fight before the Russians joined them. Napoleon did not wait for France to be invaded. He marched into Germany to meet his enemies. And long before the Russians could arrive to help them, the Austrians were shut up in the town of Ulm.

Ulm is a town of Würtemberg, one of the states of the German Empire. The German Empire, like the British Empire, is made up of several different states, but in a very different way. The British Empire is made up of four home countries—England, Scotland, Ireland, and Wales—and a great many colonies and dependencies. But in none of these states except in India are there any kings or princes under the King. In Britain there is only one king. There is no longer, as there used to be, a separate King of Scotland, or of Ireland, and although the eldest son of our King is called the Prince of Wales, it is only a title. He holds no court in Wales.

In Germany, however, it is quite different. The German Empire now consists of twenty-two states over which kings and princes rule, three states which are republics, and Alsace-Lorraine, which is an imperial province. And over the whole of these states and their kings is the Emperor.

Prussia is the largest of these states, and the King of Prussia is also Emperor of Germany. Each king or prince rules in his own country in things which matter only to his own country. But things which matter to the whole empire are settled by the Reichstag, as the German Parliament is called.

The Reichstag is held at Berlin, the capital of Prussia. Under its control are the Post Office, the army, and the navy. So none of the kings or princes of the empire can declare war, or make treaties with any other country, on his own account. That is done by the Reichstag. In its hands are also the railways, for in Germany these are ruled by Government, not by private people as with us.

In the time of Napoleon, however, the German Empire had not yet been formed. Most of the German states, and others besides, were part of the Holy Roman Empire, which had been founded by Charlemagne a thousand years before. The title of Emperor over this empire did not descend from father to son, but the princes met together on the death of the Emperor and chose another from among their number. At this time the Austrian Archduke, Francis, was Emperor. And although the Emperors had at one time been very powerful, now, in the time of Napoleon, they had become very feeble.

CHAPTER XXX

FROM ULM TO VIENNA

Some of the German states sided with Napoleon in this new quarrel which had begun. Others tried to be neutral. But Napoleon cared little for that, and he marched across their lands when it suited him.

The Austrian leader, Mack, although he was not cowardly, was stupid and unlucky, and now, as you know, Napoleon had succeeded in shutting him up in Ulm.

Like so many other countries, Germany may be divided into highland and lowland. Nearly all the north is a flat, level plain. Nearly all the south is hilly. Würtemberg, of which state Ulm is now the second town, lies in the hilly part. Here are the Black Forest Mountains, so called from the dark forests of fir trees with which they are covered.

Most of the German rivers rise in the mountains of the south and flow northward. The slope of the land is very slight, so they flow slowly, and are therefore good for navigation. This is of great importance in a country so large as Germany, as it provides a cheap way by which goods from the middle of the country may reach the sea, and also by which goods from other countries may be carried far inland.

The Danube, however, upon which Ulm stands, does not flow northward from where it rises in the Black Forest, but eastward into the Black Sea. It begins to be navigable at Ulm, although it is not of great importance as a German river, being chiefly important as the great Austria-Hungarian river. But Ulm early became of consequence as a town and fortress. For it guards some of the Alpine passes, and it is at the end of a valley connecting the Danube with the Necker, which also rises in the Black Forest and is a tributary of the Rhine. Thus it stands where roads north and south, east and west, meet and cross.

But when Napoleon besieged the town, the fortifications had long been neglected. And although there was plenty of food within the walls, Mack weakly gave in after six days' siege.

The weather had been wet and dreary, but now the sun shone out as Napoleon, surrounded by his brilliant suite, stood upon a hill outside the town to receive the Austrian officers. As the weather had been so wet, a large fire had been lit, and beside it Napoleon waited. With bowed heads and sorrowful hearts the Austrians came to lay down their swords. "Here is the unfortunate Mack," said their leader, as he first of all passed before the conqueror.

Then in mournful silence twenty-three thousand men, horse and foot, filed past. For a whole day soldiers streamed out of the gates of Ulm, some laying down their arms in moody wrath, others flinging them down in helpless indignation, that they had not been allowed by their leader to fight and die rather than weakly yield. With tears of anger they gave up their standards, which were to be sent to Paris to grace the triumph of the conqueror.

In Tyrol, in Italy, everywhere that the French and Austrians met, the Austrians were defeated, until at last a flying remnant of Mack's once splendid army took refuge in the mountains of Tyrol. There was nothing now to hinder Napoleon from marching on to Vienna, the beautiful capital of Austria.

He marched by Augsburg, one of the chief cities of South Germany. It stands upon a high moorland which stretches northward to the Danube. Here the Wertach joins with the Lech, a tributary of the Danube, and its good water-power early made Augsburg a centre of cotton and woollen factories.

Napoleon next passed on to Munich, the capital of the kingdom of Bavaria. Munich stands upon a high plain, covered in the south with pine forests and overshadowed by the mountains of

Tyrol. The broad streets are full of beautiful houses and palaces. Here many fine pictures and art treasures are gathered, and Munich is famous for its school of painting. It is also famous as a manufacturing city of artistic industries. Here beautiful glass and china are made, and works in bronze, silver, and gold. It is perhaps the most famous art city of Germany. Yet, although it may seem a curious mixture, it is almost better known for its beer. Hops grow well on all the Bavarian valleys, and Munich, having a good water-supply, and being a point at which most of the railways meet, has naturally become the centre for the manufacturing of beer.

From town to town Napoleon marched on, until, having met with but little resistance, he reached Vienna.

The Emperor Francis, knowing that Vienna could not stand a siege more than a few days, made up his mind to leave the town. And on the 13th of November, less than a month after the taking of Ulm, the French entered Vienna.

Vienna is one of the most beautiful cities on the Continent. The old fortifications have now been levelled and made into boulevards, called the Ringstrasse. There may be seen crowds of finely-dressed gay folk riding, driving, and walking. There are splendid shops, picture galleries, theatres, halls, and everything that is needed to make a brilliant capital.

But besides this Vienna has important commerce and manu-factures. It stands upon the Danube, just where that river leaves the highlands to enter the plain of Hungary. It commands passes through the Alps to Trieste, so that its trade has outlets in all directions. China, glass, silk, cotton, and woollen goods are among its manufactures.

CHAPTER XXXI

THE BATTLE OF AUSTERLITZ

Everywhere Napoleon seemed to triumph. But while he was at Vienna, living in the Emperor's beautiful palace of Schönbrunn, bad tidings came to him. He heard that the French and Spanish fleets had been utterly destroyed in the battle of Trafalgar. All hope of ever invading Britain was now gone.

"I cannot be everywhere," cried Napoleon angrily, when he heard the news.

That the French had again been defeated by sea made the Emperor more eager to win fresh fame by land. The Austrian army was shattered, but the Russians were still to beat. So from Vienna Napoleon marched out to meet them. Upon the plain of Austerlitz, not far from the town of Brunn, a great battle was fought. It has been called "the battle of the three Emperors," for there were three Emperors present—the Emperor of Germany (the Holy Roman Empire), the Emperor of Russia, and the Emperor of the French.

The morning of the 2nd December dawned cold and bleak. A thick white fog shrouded the land. But with the first streak of day both camps were astir. Through the white dimness came muffled sounds, and ghostly figures loomed and passed. Then suddenly the fog lifted, and the sun shone out in golden splendour. The French soldiers greeted it with a shout. It seemed to them as if it rose to do honour to their own Emperor, for it was the anniversary of his coronation day. "The sun of Austerlitz has risen," cried Napoleon in exultation.

In the fog the two armies had moved close to each other,

and now the fight began. It was a terrible battle, and raged all the short winter's day. "It was absolute butchery," says one who fought there. "We fought man to man."

For a time it seemed uncertain who should win, but when night fell the Russians and Austrians were flying from the field. Many lay there dead, and twenty thousand were prisoners.

Thus once more Napoleon had triumphed. And now Austria made peace with France, and the Russians marched away to their own land. This peace was called the Treaty of Pressburg, from the name of the town at which it was signed.

Pressburg at one time was the capital of Hungary, and here the kings of Hungary used to be crowned. Like Vienna, it is on the Danube, and lies pleasantly on the slope of the Little Carpathians.

By the treaty which was now signed the map of Europe was again changed. Austria gave up the Venetian lands which she had had so short a time. These were added to Italy, of which Napoleon was King. Tyrol and Voralberg were taken from Austria and given to the Elector of Bavaria, one of the German princes who had helped Napoleon, as a reward. The Elector of Würtemberg, who had also helped him, was rewarded with other lands, and both these princes were made kings.

These states and some others Napoleon now formed into the Confederation of the Rhine. "Confederation" comes from two Latin words—*con*, "together," and *feedus*, "a league." And besides his other titles, Napoleon called himself Protector of this confederation.

Although the states forming the Confederation of the Rhine had each their own ruler, they were really all under Napoleon. They had to do as he commanded them. He took away the old German laws, and the lands were ruled by the new French laws—the Code Napoleon.

By these bold and haughty deeds Napoleon had more than usurped the place of the Emperor Francis. So that beaten ruler gave up his claim to be called Emperor of the empire, for it had now become nothing but an empty title. After this he called himself Emperor of Austria only. Thus the grand empire which had lasted for more than a thousand years was shattered into bits, to be formed again and held together for a few years by the might and power of the great conqueror of Europe. But his empire, too, fell to pieces, and it was not until 1871 that the German Empire which we know today was finally formed.

Napoleon had made up his mind not only to be great himself but to make his whole family great. "I can no longer have shabby relatives," he said. "Those who will not rise with me shall no longer be of my family. I am going to make a family of kings."

So he made his brother Joseph King of Naples. His brother Louis, who had married Josephine's daughter Hortense, was made King of Holland. General Murat, who had married Napoleon's sister Caroline, was made Archduke of Berg. He made Eugene Beauharnais marry the daughter of the King of Bavaria, and a little later he made his brother Jerome marry the daughter of the King of Würtemberg. In every way Napoleon tried to make his family great, and so surround himself with splendour.

Corsicans are all proud, and Napoleon's brothers and sisters soon learned to be as haughty and arrogant as any princes of long descent. They talked to great people with ease, and were as much at home in a palace as they had been in their poor Corsican cottage. "To see your airs," said Napoleon once to his sisters, "one might think that I had received the crown from the late King my father."

At the Revolution the French had destroyed the old nobility. Napoleon now determined to make a new nobility, and to many of his bravest generals he gave the titles of prince, duke, or count. With these titles they received lands either in some conquered country or in France. So the places of the old nobles were to a great extent filled up, and the court of the Tuileries became again one of the most brilliant in Europe.

CHAPTER XXXII

WAR ONCE MORE

All this time Prussia, the greatest of the German states, had held aloof. The King was very unwilling to plunge his people into war. So he tried to be neutral and keep the peace. The King of Prussia had a large and, it was thought, well-drilled army. So that as long as Napoleon had the Russians and the Austrians to fight, he was not sorry, perhaps, that Prussia should keep peace. He even tried to bribe the King not to fight by offering to give him the electorate of Hanover. The electorate of Hanover was of course not his to give. It belonged to the King of Britain.

But now, having got rid of the Russians and the Austrians, Napoleon was very insulting to the King of Prussia. Whether he really meant to insult him, and so drive him to war, or whether he was only bent on having his own way, without caring how he hurt others, does not matter. A new war, this time between France and Prussia, soon began.

Britain, Russia, and Austria would all have helped Prussia, but King Frederick William, after having held back for so long, now rushed into war before his own plans or those of the allies were ready.

Although Prussia had a great army, many of the officers were old, and the country had been so long at peace that they had forgotten the best ways of fighting.

Napoleon, on the other hand, was always fighting, always watchful, always ready. So just as he had quickly marched against the Austrians, before the Russians had time to come to help them, now he marched against the Prussians before either they or their friends were ready.

The Prussian army entered Saxony, and forced the King of that state to join them. Saxony is one of the most important industrial states of Germany, and one of the most thickly-peopled parts of Europe. It has both iron-fields and coal-mines. And besides these two chief factory-bringing materials, it has silver, lead, copper, and tin mines. Indeed the mountains which bound Saxony in the south, and separate it from Bohemia, are called the Erz Gebirge, or Ore Mountains.

One of Germany's chief rivers, the Elbe, passes through Saxony, and is navigable all the way. So Saxony has become a great centre of factories. It has long been famous for its cotton goods. Its gently-sloping valleys make good sheep-pastures, and Saxony wool and woollen goods are famous the world over. Besides its busy factories, Saxony has beauty too, and that brings much money to the land every year. The hilly part to the south, on the borders of the Elbe, is so beautiful that it is called Saxon Switzerland.

The Prussians marched right into Saxony, and took up a position on the river Saale, a tributary of the Elbe. At Naumburg they had their stores and ammunition. Napoleon, having found this out, resolved to cross the Saale, get behind the Prussians, and cut them off from their stores.

At Saal-field, a little manufacturing town on the Saale, the first real battle took place. Here the young and gallant Prince Louis, the brother of the King, was killed. This made the Prussians very sorrowful, for the Prince was much loved.

Napoleon crossed the Saale, and with quick marches reached Naumburg, which is a quaint and interesting old town surrounded with vine-clad hills, from the grapes of which it manufactures wine.

Napoleon seized the town and blew up the gunpowder stores.

The French were now behind the Prussians, and had cut them off from their stores, as Napoleon had intended. The Prussians began to fall back. Half of the army marched northward, and half marched towards Jena, another town on the Saale. Napoleon too, with a great part of his army, marched towards the same place. And it was near Jena that the great battle of the campaign was fought.

Jena is a university town, and is interesting because Schiller and Goethe, two great German poets, both lived there. Above the town is a hill called the Landgrafenberg. Napoleon saw that this point was very important, and he ordered some cannon to be dragged up to the top.

Napoleon never troubled to think whether a thing was diffi-cult or not. If he wished anything to be done, and ordered it to be done, it had to be done, and there was an end of it. "Impossible," he said, was only to be found in the dictionary of fools. The order which he had now given was one which it was very difficult to carry out. There was no road up the Landgrafenberg by which cannon could be taken to the top. So one had to be cut through the rocks. The work was tremendously hard, and all night long the soldiers toiled, hewing and digging. But they were cheered by the sight of a short, grey-coated figure, who moved among them, speaking words of encouragement. Well they knew that grey coat and three-cornered hat. It was the Emperor himself who had come to watch. Gladdened by his presence, the men worked harder than before, wondering at the watchfulness of their leader, who seemed to take neither rest nor sleep.

When day dawned the summit of the hill was crowned with men and guns.

CHAPTER XXXIII

THE BATTLES OF JENA AND AUERSTADT

Like the dawn of Austerlitz, the dawn of Jena was shrouded in mist. Not until ten o'clock did the thick clouds roll away and the warm October sun shine out. Then, and not till then, did the Prussian leader see that he had to fight, not a small part of the French army, as he had thought, but more than eighty-three thousand men, under the great Emperor himself. He himself had scarcely more than half that number.

Once more the battle raged, and once more it ended in a great victory for Napoleon, and the Prussians were scattered in fearful rout.

On the same day, and at the same time, another battle was fought. This was at Auerstadt, about fifteen miles away. It was fought by the other half of the Prussian army, against the French under General Davoust.

King Frederick William was with this army, and at Auerstadt the Prussians far outnumbered the French. But still the result was the same, and the French won the day. The fleeing remnants of both armies met, and mingled, and fled to the nearest fortresses for safety. Thus in one day the great army of Prussia was crushed.

Troops of French soldiers now poured into Prussia from the mountains of Thuringia and Saxony, chasing the wandering fragments of the Prussian army from place to place, allowing them no time to gather or make a stand.

Prussia is for the most part a great level plain. It has no high mountains to guard its borders and form barriers against an enemy. This, as you know, is good in times of peace, as it makes trade easy but in times of war it is a misfortune. Such a country must trust to its fortresses. And now the Prussian fortresses fell one after the other into the hands of the French. Whether the garrisons were overcome with fear at Napoleon's great name, or whether some of them betrayed their country, for one reason or another the fortresses made little resistance, but gave in quickly, one after another.

Spandau, which guards the capital, Berlin, was among the first to fall. It stands where the Havel and the Spree join, and is a very strong fortress. It is in this fortress that the Germans keep a great sum of money in gold. It is called the Imperial War Fund, and is kept there to be ready at all times in case of a great war. There is also an arsenal here, where war stores are kept, and gun and gunpowder factories.

After Spandau, Stettin fell. Stettin is not only a fortress and headquarters of part of the German army, it is also an important seaport. It is the nearest seaport to Berlin, which adds to its importance. It lies at the mouth of the Oder, which is navigable right up to the Austrian frontier, so that goods can be easily carried inland. The Oder is shallow, and, unlike many of the German rivers, it is rapid. But a great deal of money has been spent to make it suitable for modern ship traffic. Breslau, one of the most important manufacturing and commercial towns of Germany, also lies upon the Oder, and Stettin forms the natural port by which its machinery, iron goods, sugar, beer, glass, and other commodities find their way to distant lands.

Stettin, too, exports a great deal of corn and sugar. The beetroot, of which this sugar is made, grows on the plains around, and in Stettin there are sugar factories. It has also shipbuilding yards and factories of machinery, for although there is no iron near, Stettin stands upon a coalfield.

Kustrin, another strongly-fortified town where the Oder and Warthe join, was next taken. Lastly Magdeburg gave in. This is a very strong fortress and busy commercial and manufacturing town. It is the centre of the German sugar trade. It is surrounded by fertile plains, where much beetroot is grown. It has splendid communication both by water and railways, and has become important as a manufacturing town, for both coal and iron can easily be brought, by rail or river, from the famous mines of Upper Silesia.

Thus all round the capital the fortresses fell, and even before Magdeburg yielded Napoleon marched in triumph to Berlin.

Berlin stands on the river Spree, in the middle of a low sandy plain. Except that it lies in the middle of the country, it does not seem to be a very good place for a great industrial city and the capital of the country, but it is both. Among its many industries are all kinds of iron goods, machinery, and china, carpets and furniture, linen, cotton, and woven goods. It also manufactures a great many "ready-made" clothes. Altogether it is one of the most important commercial and manufacturing towns of Europe.

Berlin is about a third the size of London. The German Emperor lives there, and the German Parliament, called the Reichstag, meets there. It is a beautifully ordered and clean city, and its finest street, Unter den Linden, is lined with splendid shops, hotels, and other buildings. "Unter den Linden" means "under the limes," and the street is so called from the limes with which it is planted.

Berlin is also a university town, and has a great technical school, where nearly four thousand students go to learn trades and mechanics.

CHAPTER XXXIV

THE BATTLE OF TRADE AND THE WAR OF COMMERCE

It was while Napoleon was at Berlin that he issued an order called the Berlin Decree. By this decree he forbade any country in Europe to trade with Britain. British goods, wherever they were found, were to be seized. Every British subject discovered on the Continent was to be made prisoner.

Napoleon hoped in this way to ruin British trade, and thus at last to conquer his greatest enemy. He had hoped to do this by conquering Egypt. That had failed. He had hoped to invade Britain. The battle of Trafalgar, by ruining his fleet, had made that impossible. He was now trying to conquer all Europe in order at last to conquer Britain. He meant to conquer the sea by way of the land, he said. He hoped to cut off our little islands from the rest of the world, in the matter of trade, so that in time the people, worn out by poverty and famine, would be easily crushed. A nation of shopkeepers, Napoleon scornfully called us, and by taking away our customers he thought to ruin us.

But his whole continental system, as it was called, was absurd. The countries of Europe had been so torn with wars that their manufactures, trade, and industries had suffered. Britain too had been at war; but the wars had been carried on at sea, or in foreign lands, so trade at home did not suffer so much.

Britain was at this time, perhaps more than any other, the

workshop of the world. The people on the Continent could not do without British goods. So everywhere there was smuggling, bribery, and cheating.

Some people got licences to trade with Britain. They were allowed to take shiploads of French goods to Britain, and bring back British goods in exchange. But the British did not want French goods, so these people used to buy up old damaged silks, things which were out of fashion, and that no one wanted, very cheaply. With this shipload of useless rubbish they sailed away, threw it into the sea, and came back with a load of British goods which they had bought. And things became so dear in France and all over the Continent, that these merchants got such a good price for the merchandise which they brought that they were able to spend money on buying rubbish to throw into the sea.

But in spite of all the smuggling and cheating, things which people needed every day, things which even the poorest could not do without, such as boots and shoes, woollen and cotton cloths, sugar and even medicines, became dearer and dearer. It was as if some tyrant came into a town, and, in order to ruin the shopkeepers, commanded them to shut up shop.

But in this case what are the people of the town to do. They must have food, they must have clothes. So the people of the town, seeing that they are not allowed to go openly and buy what they need, go secretly to the back doors of the shops and buy.

The shopkeepers are ready enough to sell; but they say, "This is dangerous. If we are caught we shall get into trouble, so you must pay more." So in the end it is the customers who suffer, and the shopkeepers are as well off, or better off, than before. Of course if the tyrant opened other shops just as good and as cheap as the old ones, the shop-keepers would suffer, as the people would naturally go where they could buy safely and cheaply.

But this was what Napoleon did not and could not do. There were no other shops. People had to buy from Britain.

And as things grew dearer and dearer it was the people, not the kings and rulers, who suffered most. Napoleon had driven kings from their thrones and humbled proud princes, but the people had not hated him for that. Sometimes they were glad to be rid of their old masters, and hoped for happier times under new ones. But now, when he showed that he did not care whether they were hungry and cold and miserable, so long as he gained his own ends, whole nations began to hate him.

Napoleon was a great genius. He was also a great dreamer. He carved a splendid empire for himself out of Europe, he conquered and gave away kingdoms and crowns, and beyond all that he built glorious castles in the air. What he would do he thought was done. "Impossible," as you know, he thought was a word only for fools. He did not see now that he had set himself to do the impossible. And by the Berlin Decree he perhaps dealt himself the first of many blows, which were at last to bring his splendid empire to the ground.

CHAPTER XXXV

A WINTER IN POLAND

Now, once more, Napoleon turned from the battle of trade to the battle of blood.

Crushed and dispirited, the King of Prussia tried to make peace. But Napoleon asked too much—his terms were too hard. He demanded the whole of Prussia, as far as the Vistula. Crushed though he was, the King was not ready to yield as much as that. The Russians, too, were now marching to help him. So the war went on, and it was now carried into Poland.

Poland had once been a great state and free country. But it had grown weak with quarrels within its own borders. Then the three great states around—Austria, Prussia, and Russia—had seized Poland and divided it amongst them. This was called the Partition of Poland. There were three partitions, and after the last, in 1795, there was no Poland left. Russia, indeed, had some excuse for this robbery, for part of the land had been taken from Russia by Poland years before. So the Czar was only taking back what had once belonged to himself. But Prussia and Austria had no excuse at all.

Although the Poles had no longer a country, although for ten years they had been merely the subjects of Russia, Prussia, and Austria, they had not yet forgotten that once they were free—that once they were a nation. And now, as Napoleon marched through the land, he allowed the Poles to think that he had come to conquer their tyrants and set them free again. Believing this, many of the Poles joined the French army, to fight against the Russians.

When Napoleon reached Posen, one of the most ancient Polish

towns, and one of their strongest fortresses, he was welcomed as a liberator. The streets were decorated, and he entered under an archway bearing the words, "To the Liberator of Poland."

The march through Poland was terrible. As a general rule, it had been the custom to stop fighting during winter, and begin again in the spring. But Napoleon bound himself by no such rules. So, through rain, sleet, and snow, over roads knee-deep in mud, the army moved on. The sufferings of the soldiers were great. Their boots and clothes were worn out, and not nearly warm enough. For the winter so far north is much colder than in France. Food was hard to get, no bread was to be had, the water was muddy and bad, the houses were mere hovels, where men, cows, and pigs all lived together. "And this is what the Poles have the impudence to call a country," said the French soldiers in disgust. "In Poland we have found a fifth element," said Napoleon; "it is mud."

Thus, fighting and marching, in cold, wet, and hunger, the army passed the Vistula. The Vistula is the great river of Poland, and with its tributaries is one of the great trade rivers of Europe. Much of the wood, grain, flax, and hemp from the Russian forests and steppes finds an outlet by this river.

Now at last, seeing that his men were utterly worn out, Napoleon consented to rest. He took up his headquarters at Warsaw, the capital of the province. Warsaw stands upon a coal and iron field, and besides being beautifully situated above the banks of the river, it is an important commercial town. It has a great many manufactures, among which are machinery and electroplate; and it exports much flax and wheat from the Russian plains.

The French army found quarters in the little villages along the banks of the Vistula, in a line stretching almost to the German town of Danzig, at its mouth.

The Vistula is both a German and a Russian river, and Danzig, although a German town, gets much of its importance from the quantities of wheat which it exports from Poland and West Russia. It is also the out-port for the manufactures of Warsaw and Lodz, which is the chief manufacturing town of Poland. But

Danzig is not merely a seaport. It has manufactures of its own, and is one of the chief commercial cities of northern Europe. It is also a garrison town.

Napoleon's weary soldiers were only allowed about a month's rest. For the Russians, more used to the bitter cold than the French, began to make ready for battle as soon as the swamps and marshes, hardened by frost, made it once more possible for horses and cannon to pass.

At a little place called Preuss Eylau, not far from Königsberg, a terrible battle took place. Königsberg is a strong fortress, the headquarters of part of the German army, a university town, and an important seaport. At this university the famous German philosopher Kant used to teach. He is called the "Sage of Königsberg," and is buried here.

Königsberg does great trade with Russia in wheat. It also exports much wood and flax, both of which grow well in the plains of East Russia. It is, too, the headquarters of the amber industry. Amber is found all along the Baltic shores from Pillau to Grosz Hubenicken. This part is known as the amber coast. After a storm the shore is often strewn with amber, but amber-gathering is a royal monopoly, and people may not even pick up pieces on the shore. Amber is a kind of antediluvian gum formed from vegetable juices. Besides what is found upon the shore there are amber mines, the chief being at Palmnicken. The ancients used to prize amber very highly, and think that it had magic powers, such as guarding people from being poisoned. Now it is chiefly used for cigarette-holders and pipe mouthpieces.

All the plain of East Prussia, and indeed all the shore of the Baltic, is covered with hundreds of tiny lakes. The land is very flat, but, drained by these lakes, it is dry, and marshes are unknown. But on the bitter February day on which the battle of Preuss Eylau was fought, the lakes were frozen so hard that the men fought upon the ice as upon the land. The day was dark and lowering. Heavy clouds covered the grey sky, a bitter wind drove the frozen snow, stinging the faces of the hungry, ill-fed men, who the night before had supped on nothing but potatoes.

Yet in the midst of all this misery and discomfort both sides fought with a terrible, brutal courage. "The Russians fought like bulls," said the French. Their famous Cossack horsemen charged, and wheeled, and charged again. Cannon roared, muskets cracked and rattled. And amid the screams and horrid clangour of battle, the silent white snow whirled and fell, to be trampled and reddened with the blood of fifty thousand men. At last the short winter's day was over, and darkness covered the dreadful field, which in the morning had lain so white and unstained.

Both sides claimed the victory. But indeed it was only a useless slaughter. "What a massacre!" cried a French officer, as next day he rode across the field. "What a massacre, and without result!"

CHAPTER XXXVI

THE PEACE OF TILSIT

After the battle of Preuss Eylau, both armies were so shattered that until the winter passed there was little more fighting. Napoleon even tried to make peace with King Frederick William, offering him this time much better terms than before. But the King answered that he could only make a peace which would include the Czar of Russia; so no peace was made.

With the coming of summer, the struggle began once more. After some fierce fighting, the war came to an end with a battle fought near the little town of Friedland, on the river Alle, about twenty-six miles from Königsberg,

From dawn to dark the battle lasted. The Russians fought fiercely and well. But Napoleon, as he rode about among his cheering, saluting men, cried again and again, "To-day is a lucky day. It is the anniversary of Marengo." So, roused by the memory of that great fight, the French fought with double courage. At last the Russian army, broken and dismayed, fled across the Pregel, followed closely by the pursuing French. Then, driven still at the sword's point, day by day they fled, in utter rout, until they passed the Nieman. Behind this broad river they found shelter from their foes.

Upon the one bank lay the remains of the Russian army, upon the other the French. And now that his army was shattered, the Czar sought for peace. And Napoleon, for many reasons, was ready to listen.

In the middle of the Nieman, opposite the town of Tilsit, a gaily-decorated and curtained raft was moored. Over it floated the eagle of France and the eagle of Russia, Here the two Emperors met and embraced, like brothers rather than enemies. They then went within the curtains and talked for a long time, no one being near to hear what was said. But when they came out again they seemed more friendly than before.

After this meeting the town of Tilsit, which is in Prussia, but only a few miles from the Russian frontier, was declared neutral, and both Emperors went to live there, and held their courts each in a different part of the town.

Now, instead of the horror of war, the town was full of gaiety. There were riding parties, dinners, and balls. And the Emperors, who a few days before had been bitter enemies, seemed to have become the best of friends.

The Emperor of Russia was young and handsome. He was full of splendid dreams, and eager to be great. Napoleon too was young—he was only thirty-seven, and already he was the greatest conqueror, soldier, and statesman in the world. He was often fierce, hard, and cruel; but when he chose he could seem friendly and lovable. He conquered men and women as he conquered peoples. Now he won the heart of the young Czar. "I never had more prejudices against any one than against him," he said "but after three-quarters of an hour of talk they all vanished as a dream. Would that I had seen him sooner."

The poor King of Prussia was asked to come to Tilsit from Memel, where he had taken refuge after the battle of Friedland. Memel is the most easterly port in Prussia, and it is the centre of the Baltic timber trade. It was the last fortress left to the King of Prussia.

Napoleon, who treated the Czar so kindly, treated the King of Prussia very coldly. He and his Queen, who came with him, were not allowed to live in Tilsit. They had to put up with a little mill-house outside the town. Napoleon tried in many ways to make the Prussian King and Queen feel that they were crushed and beaten enemies. It was only out of friendship to the Czar, he said, that the King had been asked to Tilsit at all. And in the drawing up of the treaty no pity for him was shown. By it Frederick William lost half his states. Part of these Napoleon made into a new kingdom, called Westphalia, which he gave to his brother Jerome.

Queen Louisa of Prussia was a very beautiful woman. She was brave too, and loved her country, and had encouraged her people to fight against Napoleon. So he hated her, and she as truly hated him, for having conquered them. It was hard for this proud Queen to meet a man, whom she thought of as an upstart and a brigand, as an equal. Yet now, for the sake of her country, she tried to please him. She knew that much of Prussia was lost, but when she heard that Napoleon meant to take the fortress of Magdeburg she was very sad, and tried hard to persuade him to let her keep it.

One day at dinner Napoleon admired a rose which the Queen wore.

"Will your Majesty take it in exchange for Magdeburg?" she said, holding it out to him.

Napoleon bent over her hand, saying pretty things about its beauty. The Queen's eyes filled with tears, but the Emperor pretended not to see them. He did not take the rose, but kept Magdeburg.

Prussia was now little more than a province of France, her King little more than a vassal. And both the King of Prussia and the Czar of Russia were forced by the treaty of Tilsit to agree to Napoleon's continental system, and shut out British traders from their lands.

Then, after everything was arranged, Napoleon returned to Paris.

CHAPTER XXXVII

INTO PORTUGAL

All this time, in spite of the Berlin Decree and the continental system, Portugal went on trading with Britain. Now, soon after Napoleon returned to Paris, he sent a message to the Prince Regent of Portugal, telling him that he must stop trading with Britain, must seize all British goods and property in Portugal, and declare war with Britain. If he did not do all this, Napoleon threatened that he would declare war with Portugal.

Portugal is only a little country, quite unable to stand against such a powerful conqueror as Napoleon. So the Prince Regent agreed to all that was asked, except the seizing of British goods. That he would not do. So Napoleon prepared to fight.

If you look on the map, you will see that Spain and Portugal together form a broad peninsula, surrounded on all sides by the Atlantic and the Mediterranean, except where it is cut off from France by the high mountains of the Pyrenees.

France at this time had hardly any navy. Napoleon had not enough ships in which to send his troops by sea. To make war on Portugal he would have to pass through Spain. So he now made a secret treaty with the King of Spain by which his troops were to be allowed to pass through that country. And when by the help of Spanish soldiers he had conquered Portugal, he promised to divide it with Spain.

Spain and Portugal are naturally and geographically one. The mountains of Portugal are merely the continuations of the mountains of Spain, and the frontier between the two lands is quite unprotected.

The whole of the peninsula, both of Spain and Portugal, is a high tableland, ribbed across and ringed around by still higher mountains.

The rivers of Portugal, too, are the rivers of Spain. They are mostly long, passing through the whole breadth of the peninsula. But as they rise high, they are for the most part rapid, narrow, and winding, and of little use in commerce. "The rivers of Spain," it has been said, "have long names, narrow channels, and little water." The chief of them are the Douro, the Tagus, and the Guadiana. But it is only after they reach Portugal that they become navigable and of any use for trade. In summer-time, when in Spain they are almost dried up, in Portugal they are still full of water.

But although the rivers are not of much use in commerce, they are very valuable for watering the land.

As a rule, an island has a much moister climate than a continent. It also has a more even climate. The Iberian Peninsula, as Spain and Portugal are called, is almost an island. Yet inland it has one of the driest climates in Europe, and inland the extremes of heat and cold are very great.

For this there are one or two reasons. The tableland is so high, and it comes so near the coast, that the rain-laden winds from the Atlantic are robbed of all their moisture long before they reach the centre of Spain. The winds from the south blow over the dry Sahara, and here the Mediterranean is so narrow that they cannot gather much moisture from it. Another reason for the dryness of the climate is that such forests as there used to be in Spain have been recklessly cut down, and no new trees have been planted to take their place. That makes the climate drier than it need be, for trees gather and hold the rain in their wide-spreading branches and roots. Portugal, therefore, and the fringes of Spain, gather all the moisture, and the centre of Spain is left dry. In summer the high tableland is scorched by the sun, in winter it is swept by bitter winds, and much of it has become bleak and barren desert. Around this arid plain is a circle of rich and fertile land, gleaming with the gold, and green, and purple of wheat-field, vineyard, and orchard.

The kingdom of Portugal was at this time ruled by a Regent. The Queen, Maria I., was mad, and her son, Prince John, ruled for her. Now when the Regent heard that Napoleon was gathering an army to fight him, he made up his mind to leave the war to Britain, and take his poor, mad mother away to Brazil, which was then a Portugese colony. So, one wet and cold November morning the Queen and Prince and many of the nobles set sail, leaving a sad and mourning people behind.

Meanwhile Napoleon had gathered a large army at Bayonne, a strongly-fortified town close to the Pyrenees, but on the French side of them. This army, under Marshal Junot, now came march-ing quickly through Spain to Lisbon, the capital of Portugal. They crossed the Pyrenees, which, next to the Alps, are the highest mountains in Europe. Over the wind-swept plain they came, across rivers, down rugged valleys, by muddy tracks which could scarcely be called roads. The men grew weary, but Junot urged them onward. The land was barren and bare, and they had often hardly enough to eat. For, as was usual with Napoleon's armies, they carried no supplies with them, but trusted to finding what they needed in the land they passed through. "I will not have the march kept back because of supplies," said the Emperor. "Twenty thousand men can find food anywhere, even in a desert." Most of the soldiers in this army were mere boys, raw recruits, unused to such hardships. Many of them dropped out of the ranks, overcome with weariness, and were left by the wayside to die.

At last, little more than a month after they had set out from Bayonne, they arrived, footsore, hungry, and ragged, at Lisbon, too late. The ship carrying the Queen and Prince was already far out to sea.

CHAPTER XXXVIII

INTO SPAIN

From its high tableland, the shores of Portugal slope sharply to the sea. The coast is very unbroken, there are few bays or islands, the tides and currents are rapid and dangerous, and all this, together with its narrow, swift rivers, gives the country few good harbours. But of these Lisbon is the best. It is a really fine natural harbour, and its trade is important, as it is a port of call for British and continental steamers on their way to and from Africa and Brazil.

Lying upon the grand bay of the Tagus, Lisbon is in situation one of the most beautiful cities in Europe. Like Rome, it is built upon hills, and terrace upon terrace, its dazzling white houses, red-roofed and nestling in green gardens, rise above the blue waters. "He who has not seen Lisbon does not know what beauty is," say the Portuguese. Yet this fair city, little more than a hundred and fifty years ago, was laid in ruins. On All Saints' Day, 1755, it was wrecked by a fearful earthquake. Nearly every one was in church when the walls began to rock and fall, and thousands were crushed to death as they knelt in prayer. A great tidal wave swept in from the sea, and the roar of the waves and the crash of falling houses mingled with shrieks of terror and pain. The air grew dark with dust, fire broke out, and, driven by a fierce wind, spread rapidly from house to house, destroying what the earthquake had spared. Many dirty and dark alleys were destroyed, and when the town was built again, the streets were made broad and regular, and now Lisbon is one of the cleanest towns of the Continent.

Beside Lisbon, the only other important town in Portugal is Oporto. It is from this town that the whole country takes its name, and it is also from it that the wine "port" is named. Port is made from the grapes which grow in the valley of the Douro, upon a grey and seemingly barren soil.

Now French uniforms were to be seen in every street in Lisbon, and soon they began to take possession of the whole country. There was little fighting. Had there been in the Portuguese army even a handful of bold and resolute men, it might have gone ill with Junot's raw and worn-out soldiers. But there were none such.

Everywhere the French pulled down the royal arms of Portugal, and set up those of Napoleon. Many of the Portuguese soldiers were sent away to France, so that they might not have a chance of fighting for their country even if a leader should appear. The Portuguese people were made to pay great sums of money to the conqueror, who declared that the House of Braganza—that is, the royal house of Portugal—had ceased to reign.

And while all this was happening, French troops kept on pouring into Spain, in far greater numbers than were needed to conquer little Portugal.

"Write descriptions of all the provinces through which you pass," said Napoleon, as he sent them away. "Describe the roads and the nature of the land. Send me sketches, that I may see the distance of the villages, the nature of the country, and the resources of the land." All this was not necessary if he merely intended to pass through the land to reach Portugal. No, he had another design, far greater than the conquest of Portugal, in his mind.

The Spanish people had been told to treat these French soldiers as friends, but not to allow them into any of the fortresses. Napoleon, however, determined to get possession of the fortresses. And he did so, often by treachery. At one place, for instance, leave was asked to bring all the sick into the fort. This was granted. But no sooner were the seemingly sick men carried within the walls than they sprang up, fully armed, overpowered the garrison, and were soon in possession of the fortress. By such tricks the French had soon many of the strongest places of Spain in their hands.

Spain at this time was badly ruled. The King, Charles IV., was old and foolish. All the power was in the hands of the Queen, who was not a good woman, and of Manuel Godoy, her favourite. He was not a good man, but he had been given the beautiful name of the Prince of Peace, because at one time he had helped to make a peace with France.

The King's eldest son, Ferdinand, hated Godoy, and quarrelled with him. So the court of Spain was full of strife. Now both sides appealed to Napoleon for help. It was rather like mice putting their heads into a cat's mouth. The King and Queen began to think so, and they decided to run away, as the Queen and Prince of Portugal had done, and take refuge from all their troubles in America.

The royal family were then at the palace of Aranjuez, about thirty miles south of Madrid. They began to prepare for their long journey to Seville, where they intended to set sail.

But when the people found out what they meant to do, they were very angry, and broke out into a riot. They burst into Godoy's palace in search of the man they hated. They could not find him, so they wreaked their vengeance on the beautiful furniture and pictures, leaving the palace a waste of splinters and rags. Meanwhile, he, trembling in fear, was hiding in a roll of matting in the attic.

There for two days he remained, and at last, driven by hunger, he crept out. He hoped to escape unseen, but at once he was seized, and would have been torn to pieces by the angry mob, had not Prince Ferdinand begged for his life.

CHAPTER XXXIX

JOSEPH BONAPARTE, KING OF SPAIN

Now the weak old King of Spain, trembling for the life of his friend, the Prince of Peace, decided to give up the throne to his son Ferdinand. He hoped in this way to quiet the riot. But the people, when they heard the news, went mad with joy, and to show it, they burned and sacked the houses belonging to Godoy, his friends, and relatives, while they proclaimed Ferdinand King with shouting and cheering.

But their joy was shortlived. Almost at once the old King began to be sorry that he had given up the crown, and wanted it back again. And meanwhile French troops were closing in round Madrid.

Soon it became known that Napoleon himself was coming. And hearing that his father and mother were going to meet the Emperor, Ferdinand resolved to go too, and lay his case before him. The people were very unwilling that he should go, for they felt sure that some evil would befall their young King. At one place, as he travelled through the land, they cut the traces of his horses, thinking to make him give up his intention. But he went on.

As there was still no sign of Napoleon when Ferdinand reached the border, he crossed into France, and met him at Bayonne.

There too came the old King, the Queen, and Manuel Godoy. Beyond their own borders, surrounded by French soldiers, they were Napoleon's prisoners. They had of free will, it seemed, walked into the trap.

And now Napoleon told them that it was useless to quarrel about who should be King of Spain, as he wanted the throne for one of his own family. "The House of Bourbon has ceased to reign," he said, in his usual grand way.

What could the poor Spanish Kings do? The whole country was in the hands of the French, and they themselves prisoners in a foreign land. So at the bidding of Napoleon they signed away the crown and throne of Spain.

Without striking a blow, Napoleon had added two more kingdoms to his conquests; and with Spain went all her rich colonies in the West. But it had been done by base treachery. Even he himself long after said, "The whole thing wears an ugly look since I have fallen."

It is said that Napoleon now sent for his brother Lucien, with whom he had quarrelled, and offered him the throne of Spain. But Lucien would not come. He thought himself happier living quietly at home than sitting upon such a dangerous throne. Louis Bonaparte, King of Holland, too, refused the throne. Then, without telling him why he was wanted, Napoleon sent for Joseph, who was already King of Naples.

Joseph, who had always allowed himself to be bullied by Napoleon, came. And when he reached Bayonne he was much surprised to find that he was "King of Spain and the Indies."

Napoleon then made General Murat King of Naples, in place of Joseph.

But the people of Spain would have no Bonaparte to reign over them. The Spaniards are the most polite and courteous of men. They are idle and indolent too, seldom showing any energy. But now they were thoroughly roused. To a man they rebelled. From every town and village they flocked, ready to fight for their freedom and their King.

Meanwhile the new King Joseph, guarded by French troops, came to live in the capital.

Except that Madrid lies nearly in the middle of Spain, it has nothing to make it a good capital. It is the highest capital in

Europe, standing upon an enormous, almost barren and uncultivated, treeless tableland. In summer it is unbearably hot; in winter it is wet, bleak, and cold. In summer the little river on which it stands is a dry bed, and never at any time is it of the slightest use for trade.

Yet, being the capital, the residence of the King, and the seat of Government, Madrid has become a bright and gay city, and the centre of the few rail-ways which cross the peninsula. Its streets are wide and planted with trees, and it has one of the finest picture-galleries in Europe, or indeed in the world.

The Spaniards are a courteous and polite people, but now they received their new King in sullen silence. And as Joseph looked at the dark faces which surrounded him, he felt that he had not a friend among them.

Everywhere there was fighting. Yet so sure was Napoleon that now everything would go on in Spain just as he wished, that he left Bayonne, and set out on a tour through some of the French towns.

Before he left, he wrote a long letter to his officers, full of proud confidence. "There is nothing to fear in Castille or Leon," he wrote. "There is nothing to fear in Aragon or Catalonia. There is nothing to fear about communications between Burgos and Bayonne. General Dupont holds the only point of danger, but with twenty-five thousand men he has more than he needs, with which to command great results."

But even as Napoleon wrote, messengers were speeding northward, over dreadful roads, which are to this day the worst in Europe, with the news that General Dupont and all his men had surrendered to the Spaniards at Bailen.

At last the spell was broken, and defeat, not victory, followed the French. Napoleon, the conqueror of kings, was not yet the conqueror of peoples. And now a people not easily moved had been roused to wrath against him. All through enslaved Europe the news from Spain sent a stir of hope. The hearts of whole nations beat again with the thought that perhaps they might yet be freed from tyranny.

Napoleon was furiously angry. "Could I have expected that from Dupont!" he cried. "A man I loved! He had no other way to save his soldiers? Better, far better, to have died with arms in their hands. You can always supply the place of soldiers. Honour alone, once lost, can never be regained."

CHAPTER XL

THE MAID OF SARAGOSSA

The French had taken the fortress of Barcelona by treachery. Now the Spaniards besieged them there. Barcelona has been called the Manchester of Spain. It is the second city of the kingdom, and not only is it a manufacturing town, but it lies amidst many other busy industrial towns, which is unusual in Spain; for it is a country very far behind in trade and commerce.

Although Spain is more rich in minerals than any other country in Europe, its mines are little worked. This is partly owing to the character of the people, who lack energy. They prefer to beg in the sunshine, rather than work for their daily bread in the darkness of the earth. Indeed the mines which are worked are chiefly in the hands of British, French, and German traders.

Among its minerals Spain has coal; but it is little worked, partly because both road and water-ways are bad, and it is difficult to distribute the coal over the country to the places where it is needed. For this reason manufactures are few.

But coal can be brought fairly easily from the chief coalfield, near Oviedo, along the valley of the Ebro, to Barcelona. And it is in Catalonia, as the province in which Barcelona lies is called, that the people are most energetic and hardy. It is also the most thickly peopled part of Spain. And here, in the midst of waving palm-trees, vine and orange groves, rise the tall chimneys of cotton and woollen factories. Besides being a manufacturing

The Maid of Saragossa

town, Barcelona is the best seaport of Spain. A quarter of all the foreign trade passes through it.

While the Spaniards besieged this busy town of Barcelona, the French besieged Gerona. Gerona is a quaint and interesting town, and one of Spain's chief fortresses. It held out for seven months against thirty-five thousand French. There was only a small garrison within the walls. But men, and women too, fought, and not till all their ammunition was gone, not until they were gaunt and starving skeletons, did they give in.

Near Gerona there are forests of cork-trees, for which Spain is famous. The best champagne-bottle corks in all the world come from Gerona. Cork is the outer bark of a kind of evergreen oak. When the bark is stripped from the trees, it grows again in eight or ten years. And each time it grows better. The first bark is taken from the tree when it is about fifteen or twenty years old. This is very coarse, and is generally used only for rustic work. It is called virgin cork. A cork-tree will live, and go on bearing bark, for about a hundred years.

Besides these towns, Saragossa, the central city of the valley of the Ebro, was besieged. It is a truly Spanish town. Many of the streets are winding and narrow, and the people still dress in the picturesque Spanish costume. It is a university town, and has a beautiful cathedral, and since railways have been built, it has begun to be busy and prosperous.

But Saragossa lies in a barren region. The whole of Aragon, shut in by mountains from the rain-laden winds, is treeless and dreary, except here and there, in a kind of oasis, where fruit-trees and vines grow in the deep valleys of some of the larger streams.

The fortifications of Saragossa were poor; but the hearts of the people were stout. Day by day they held out, the women fighting beside the men. One woman, named Maria Augustin, became famous, and was called "the Maid of Saragossa." She fought beside her lover, helping him to fire the cannon of which he was in charge, and when he fell dead, she still went on fighting and worked the cannon herself.

Hunger and disease fought, too, against the brave defenders. Still they held out. The French at last gained possession of a convent which was almost within the walls. Their leader then sent a summons to the town. It was short and sharp. "Headquarters, St. Engracia. Surrender," was all it said.

The reply was as sharp. "Headquarters, Saragossa. War to the knife." At last, hearing of the defeat at Bailen, where Dupont and all his men had laid down their arms to the Spaniards, the French gave up the siege of Saragossa and marched away, "Foil'd by a woman's hand, before a battered wall."

Afterwards, when the war of liberation was over, Maria Augustin received medals, as did other soldiers, in reward for her bravery, and her portrait was bought by people all over Europe. It was long ere the name of the Maid of Saragossa was forgotten.

Saragossa was saved for once, but the French came again; and again the town was besieged. At last the French broke through the defences. But even then the town would not yield. From street to street the people fought. Every house was a fortress, and had to be stormed separately. At last, after three weeks of this street fighting, worn out by hunger and famine, the gallant defenders gave in.

CHAPTER XLI

THE COURT AT ERFURT

With fighting going on all around him, King Joseph did not stay long in Madrid. Ten days after he had arrived there, he left again. The night before he left, two thousand servants deserted the palace; nearly all his courtiers went too. So he fled, almost alone, to Vittoria, beyond the Ebro.

And now Spain was not left to fight her war of liberation unaided. Britain had been at war with Spain. In the battle of Trafalgar the fleet of Spain had been destroyed with that of France. "But the kingdom thus nobly struggling against the usurpation and tyranny of France can no longer be considered as the enemy of Great Britain," said King George. "It is recognised by me as a natural friend and ally."

So British troops were sent to help the Spaniards in their struggle. And thus began for us the war which we call the Peninsular War.

The Portuguese, taking heart at the example of their neighbours, rose too. It was in Portugal that the British, under Sir Arthur Wellesley, first landed, in the beginning of August 1808. By the end of that month the French were beaten out of the country, and the war was carried into Spain.

It will be impossible to follow all this war. The story of it belongs to another place, especially as Napoleon himself was very little with his soldiers in Spain. The Spaniards were not always victorious, even after the British came to help them. Both they and the Portuguese were divided into parties who did not always work or fight together. Yet the French suffered many a blow.

But meantime, even while this great struggle was going on, Napoleon was turning his eyes and thoughts to still greater conquests. He had dreams of conquering Turkey, and from there passing on through Asia to India, and at last "Britain would tremble and bow the knee before the Continent."

But for this the friendship and help of the Czar was needed. So now Napoleon arranged a meeting with Alexander, in order to renew the friendship of Tilsit, which seemed to have cooled. That, indeed, was scarcely wonderful, for Napoleon's continental system was very hard on the Russian people.

Napoleon wanted, too, to show all the world how powerful he was, and frighten Europe, especially Austria and Prussia, with a display of this power, so that if they had any thoughts of rebellion, they would give them up.

The meeting took place at Erfurt, in the hilly country of Thuringia, which, like Saxony, has many small industrial towns, although the mining industries are by no means so important. Erfurt is perhaps most interesting as the place where Luther was a monk, and the cell in which he lived for about three years is still to be seen.

Now the quiet old town was brilliant with uniforms, and the streets made noisy with the tramp of feet, and the thunder of saluting guns. For Napoleon gathered round him a court of all his vassal kings. There were so many of them that they were quite common. "Be quiet; it is only a king," an officer would say, when his men began to cheer some splendid procession, thinking that one of the Emperors was coming.

During the day the two Emperors talked, and dined, and rode together. In the evening there were balls and parties. Then, having made a grand display, Alexander and Napoleon said goodbye to each other, the one riding off to his capital, St. Petersburg, the other hurrying to fight in Spain. And silence once more fell upon Erfurt.

A few days after he left Erfurt, Napoleon was at Vittoria. He was no longer the brilliant Emperor, but a soldier, eager for war and victory. Great preparations had been made to receive him.

But instead of going to his palace, he went into the first inn he came to, called for maps, and was soon deep in plans for ending the war.

The Spaniards, rejoicing in their first victories, had thought to carry all before them. But now they had the greatest soldier in all the world against them. And with him had come many fresh troops.

From Vittoria to Burgos, and on ever nearer and nearer to Madrid, the French advanced, sweeping all before them. Through olive-groves and vineyards and wheat-fields, or again by desolate valleys and barren hills, they marched, until they reached the Sierra de Guadarrama, the hills which guard Madrid on the north.

Here, at the pass Somosierra, the Spaniards were strongly posted. But Napoleon charged up the pass, captured the guns, and the Spaniards fled, some to Segovia, others to Talavera.

The way to Madrid was now unguarded, and next morning, 2nd December, the French troops appeared before it. Two days later Madrid surrendered.

CHAPTER XLII

CORUNNA

For a few weeks Napoleon stayed in Madrid, altering the laws, issuing proclamations, and making plans like a conqueror. But Spain was still unconquered. In the north, in the province of Galicia, were British troops under a gallant Scotsman, Sir John Moore. At Seville, the capital of Andalusia, lay a Spanish force.

Seville is one of the most delightful towns in Spain, as well as one of the most prosperous. For with careful dredging the sand has been cleared away from the channel of the Guadalquiver, upon which it lies, so that steamers can come right up to Seville. It has silk factories, and trade in fruit and tobacco, and it lies in a region of gardens.

Here roses blossom all winter, and our spring flowers bloom in January. Here are vineyards, orange, olive, and cork groves, and fertile wheat fields. Here the sky is always blue. In winter, cold, frost, and snow are almost unknown, but the summer is scorchingly hot.

But more than its present prosperity, it is the beauty of its buildings and the history of its past that make Seville interesting. Here is the famous Alcazar Palace of the ancient Moorish kings, and the Giralda, once the prayer-tower of a Moorish mosque. For Spain was once conquered by the Moors, and they gave to Spain some of its most splendid palaces. The most famous is the Alhambra at Granada.

Seville was the birthplace of Murillo and Velasquez, two famous Spanish artists. It was here that Columbus was received in state when he returned from his first voyage of discovery. And after the discovery of America, Seville became very famous and prosperous, although later it lost that prosperity, which it is now only recovering.

Not far from Seville lie the Rio Tinto and Tharsis copper mines, in one of the richest mineral districts of Spain. These mines were known to the Phoenicians and to the Romans, and are still among the most important copper mines in the world. They are now in the hands of British and German traders. All round are villages where the miners live. It is a desolate region, covered with slag and refuse, where nothing will grow. Every green thing is killed by copper fumes and the smoke from furnaces.

At Valentia, upon the eastern coast, there was fighting too. The province of Valentia is full of barren hills and fertile valleys. All kinds of fruit and grains and fibres grow here, two or three crops being gathered one after the other every year. Orange-trees often have ripe fruit, green fruit, and blossom all at the same time.

Much of this fertility is due to the splendid system of watering by canals, which the Moors made, when they possessed the land. Indeed it is chiefly where these canals still exist that the land is fertile. But in many places they have been allowed to go to waste, and much of the land which was cultivated in the time of the Moors, or even in the time of the Romans, is now barren and useless. And nearly half of Spain is uncultivated, but upon the barren slopes and plains much esparto grass grows, for it likes dry heat, and will grow where other things requiring moisture cannot.

Even where the Spaniards do till the soil they do it in very old-fashioned ways. The land is generally dug and hoed by hand, and where ploughs are used, they are old-fashioned wooden ones drawn by oxen. The crops when ripe are cut down by sickles, the grain is trodden out by oxen, and winnowed by hand. Such a thing as machinery for farm work is unknown. The carts are drawn by oxen or mules, and in many places the roads are so bad that no cart can pass over them, and goods have to be carried upon the backs of mules in panniers.

Napoleon meant to send armies under different generals to

every part of Spain where there was a rising. He himself meant to march into Portugal. But he now heard that Sir John Moore was marching towards Salamanca, so he resolved to go to meet him and crush him.

Sir John had hoped to join with other British and Spanish troops. But in this he had been disappointed. His army alone was not strong enough to meet Napoleon's forty thousand. So as Napoleon advanced Sir John retreated through the bleak hills of Galicia to Corunna.

The weather, which had been good, now became wet and cold. But both armies marched rapidly over the rough and almost unmade roads. Napoleon made quite sure of trapping the British. "Say in the newspapers that thirty-six thousand British are surrounded," he wrote to "King" Joseph. But the British were by no means surrounded, and again and again, as the retreat went on, the French were repulsed.

At Astorga Napoleon suddenly left the army. Giving his general, Soult, the command to "drive the British into the sea," he galloped away towards Paris. For he had ill news. Austria was arming to fight, and Russia was like to join. Perhaps, too, Napoleon was glad of an excuse to leave Spain for it did not seem so certain that this campaign against the British was going to succeed, and it might bring but little glory to his name.

By this time the British army on its retreat to Corunna had become almost a rabble. The men were worn out, but they hated to retreat, and wanted to fight. So discipline gave way, and at times it seemed as if the army would become little more than an armed mob.

At last, after a journey of two hundred and fifty miles, Corunna was reached. But there were no ships awaiting the British soldiers to carry them home. So for a few days Sir John spent the time bringing his disordered troops into order again, and making ready to fight the French should they appear.

At last the British ships arrived in the bay. But the French too arrived, and made ready to fight. And on the 15th of January the battle of Corunna took place.

The French were beaten, but the victory cost the life of the British general. "I have always wished to die like this," he said as he lay dying. "I hope the people of England will be satisfied. I hope my country will do me justice. It is a great satisfaction to know that we have beaten the French." And thus, if not quite victorious, at least pointing the way to victory, this brave and gentle soldier died.

And there on his last battlefield Sir John was laid in a soldier's grave. Next day his men sailed homeward, for the French were too badly beaten to try to hinder them any more.

CHAPTER XLIII

THE BATTLES OF ASPERN-ESSLING AND WAGRAM

The Peninsular War was by no means over. The Duke of Wellington, then Sir Arthur Wellesley, now took full command. It was not, however, until after five more years of fighting that the French were at last swept out of Spain and Portugal, and driven beyond the Pyrenees once more. But the story of all that belongs to British history more than to the story of Napoleon, and it is with Napoleon that we have to do.

When Napoleon arrived in Germany in April 1809, he found his army between the Danube and the Isar, stretched out in a long line from Regensburg to Augsburg. Quickly he drew his army together and advanced to meet the Austrians.

Day by day as he advanced, he fought. Day by day the Austrians were beaten and driven towards Regensburg. It was a five days' battle, each day a victory. Never had Napoleon's genius as a soldier seemed greater. Never had he been so sure and calm.

Regensburg, which Napoleon now stormed, lies upon the Danube where it becomes navigable for steamers. It rose to importance in the days when commerce was carried through the Alpine passes and along the Danube. It is still an interesting town, for there, more than in any other German town, may be seen old and beautiful houses, where the great merchants used to live six or seven hundred years ago.

A few miles down the Danube is the Walhalla, or Hall of the Chosen. This is a splendid hall built of marble, within which are placed busts of all great men belonging to the German races. This hall was not there when Napoleon stormed and took Regensburg. It was built later by Louis I., King of Bavaria, who also built a Hall of Liberation in memory of the war of freedom which was now beginning.

Napoleon, after storming Regensburg, marched into Austria, and once more took Vienna. Meanwhile it was not only the Austrians who were fighting. In Tyrol the peasants had risen under a brave leader called Hofer. In Germany, in Poland, and in Italy, everywhere, the people rose. In many places they won battles. But after all, where Napoleon led, there was the heart of the fight. And he was everywhere victorious.

The Austrian army was now on one side of the Danube and the French on the other; and it seemed as if it would be impossible for either to cross. But the Danube, which is a rapid, deep, and narrow river until it reaches Vienna, here opens out broadly, and is covered with islands. The largest of these is called Lobau. By these islands Napoleon succeeded in crossing, and took possession of two little villages on the opposite side, called Aspern and Essling.

Here for two days a fearful battle raged, called from these villages Aspern-Essling, or sometimes the battle of the Marchfield. This was one of the fiercest of Napoleon's battles, and so well did the Austrians fight that for him it was a check. Under cover of the darkness he drew his troops back to the island of Lobau. Had the Austrians followed up, perhaps the war might have ended differently from what it did. But they had lost too many men and were too weary to follow.

Both sides, indeed, were so worn out that some weeks passed without much fighting. Then Napoleon again crossed the Danube, and on the 6th of July, at Wagram, another village on the left bank, a second battle took place.

The Austrians again fought with splendid courage, and when night came, of the fifty thousand who lay dead, nearly as many were French as Austrian. It was one of the fiercest battles ever fought, and to Napoleon it counted barely a victory.

Yet for the Emperor of Austria it was enough. He was not made of the stern stuff of heroes and patriots. Once more he yielded. And on the 14th of October the treaty of Schönbrunn, so called from the name of the beautiful palace in Vienna where Napoleon was living, was signed.

By this treaty Austria lost still more land. Napoleon took for France the lands lying round the Adriatic, so that Austria had no seaport left. Parts of Upper Austria, Galicia, and Bohemia, were given to Napoleon's vassal kings to reward them for having helped him. For it must be remembered that Napoleon's great armies were not made up only of Frenchmen, but of men from every country which he had conquered, or over whose ruler he held sway.

About this time, too, Napoleon once more quarrelled with the Pope, and took all his land away from him. The Pope in return excommunicated the Emperor. Napoleon then took the Pope prisoner. He was sent to Fontainebleau, where he remained for more than three years, living in great splendour, but still a captive. Now having the Papal States, all Italy, from north to south, was under Napoleon's rule.

CHAPTER XLIV

THE EMPRESS MARIE LOUISE

After the treaty of Schönbrunn was signed, Napoleon returned to Paris.

And now one of the strangest things in his life happened. You remember that long ago, when the Emperor was a poor soldier, he had married a beautiful lady, called Josephine de Beauharnais. He had loved her very much. "To live for Josephine—that is the history of my life," he had written then. "I prize honour since you prize it; I prize victory since it pleases you."

Now glory, if not honour, was heaped upon him. He had piled victory upon victory, but he forgot what he had written as a young and eager boy. He put away his beautiful wife, and married the Duchess Marie Louise, the daughter of his late enemy the Emperor of Austria.

One reason why Napoleon did this was that his pride had grown with his power. He still loved Josephine, but he longed to have a great lady for his wife—a princess, the daughter of a long line of kings, to be the mother of his children.

Marie Louise was little more than a girl. She had hated Napoleon, and once when she heard that he had been defeated, she said that she was glad, and hoped that it would happen again. Now she came to be his wife, because her father told her, perhaps, that this marriage would help to bring peace and freedom to her country. She now became the Empress Marie Louise.

The war in the peninsula still went on, but otherwise Europe seemed to have a breathing space. Yet Napoleon did not cease adding to the realms of France.

When the Emperor made his friends and brothers kings, he expected them to obey him absolutely. He expected them to think, not first of the subjects that they had been given to rule, but first of Napoleon and of France, and then perhaps of their subjects.

Napoleon had made his brother Louis King of Holland, but for a long time now he had been very angry with him. For Louis seemed to want to rule Holland for Holland's good, and not as his brother ordered him. One of his chief misdeeds was that he set aside the continental system, and allowed his people to trade with Britain. For a long time Louis tried to resist Napoleon's orders, but at last, tired of a mere pretence of ruling, he gave up his throne, and went away to live quietly in Bohemia.

Napoleon then added Holland to France.

Holland is an absolutely flat country. Much of the land, indeed, lies below the level of the sea, and has to be protected by great dykes. The rivers, too, flowing through this flat land, and bringing down great deposits of mud, have to be guarded by dykes. So the Dutchman has a constant fight with the water for his land, and in spite of dykes and canals, much of it is still watery fen-land.

But the Dutchman is hardy and industrious. Nearly three-fourths of the country is pasture or agricultural land, and Holland is famous for horses and cattle, butter and cheese. It has manufactures too, but these, owing to the fact that Holland has no coal, are chiefly on the coast, as are all its large towns. Holland has not only no coal; it has no minerals at all, except china clay. It has therefore become famous for its china and earthenware, one kind of which we call "delf," from the town Delft, where it is made. Its chief industry is shipbuilding, but it also makes gin—often called "Hollands," or sometimes "Schiedam," from the name of the town where it is made.

Besides this, Holland has manufactures of sugar and cigars, and, as is natural from its great quantity of cattle, it has many leather and margarine factories.

Of course, since coal began to be used for manufacturing, the trade of Holland has suffered in some ways from the lack of it. But it has a fertile soil, good seaports, splendid communication inland, by canal and rail, a fine position in regard to other countries, an industrious people, and it comes next to Great Britain in its number of colonies, and so it continues to be a wealthy and prosperous country.

Besides this rich pastoral country, Napoleon annexed to France all the German coast as far as the frontier of Denmark, as well as the seaport towns of Hamburg, Bremen, and Lubeck, thus shutting out British trade entirely from the northern shores of the Continent. He gave orders that all British goods, and the goods of all British colonies, were to be seized and burned, and made laws for punishing those who traded in them. But in spite of all this, smuggling went on to a tremendous extent all over his vast empire.

CHAPTER XLV

INTO RUSSIA

On the 20th of March 1811 a little son was born to Napoleon, who at once gave him the title of King of Rome. Now with a son to follow him upon the throne, Napoleon seemed to be at the very height of his glory. "Now begins the finest epoch of my reign," he said. At forty-one he seemed to have the world at his feet. Really his downfall had begun.

The people of Russia had found Napoleon's continental system very hard, and the Czar became less and less inclined to make his people keep the Berlin Decree. As more and more British goods were allowed to pass into Russia, Napoleon grew more and more angry. There were other reasons for quarrelling, and at last war between the two rival Emperors, who had sworn to be friends at Tilsit and at Erfurt, broke out.

Napoleon decided utterly to crush his great rival, and to force all Europe over which he had control to help him.

At Dresden, the capital of the kingdom of Saxony, he gathered all his vassal kings. There, in a blaze of splendour, he dazzled the world once more. Dresden was a good place for such a display. It is a fine city, a residential place, and one of the art centres of Germany, being famous for its splendid collection of pictures. It is a manufacturing town too, being on a navigable river and in the middle of a coalfield. It has many manufactures, among which are gold and silver ornaments and artificial flowers. Dresden china, however, is not made at Dresden, but at Meissen, a little farther down the river.

For some days Dresden was gay with feasting and merry-making, with ceremonies and spectacles, then Napoleon set out once more to play his deadly game of war.

Through the land, all beautiful in the fresh greenness of early summer, under sunshine and blue skies, marched the mighty army, six hundred thousand strong. From all the states of Germany, from Prussia, Austria, Holland, Belgium, Italy, Poland, Switzerland, even from Spain and Portugal, soldiers had come to swell the stream which poured across the Niemen into Russia.

"Russia is dragged by her fate. Let us carry war into her territories, and put an end for ever to her haughty influence," said Napoleon to his army.

"Soldiers," said Alexander, "you fight for your religion, your liberty, and your native land. Your Emperor is with you; and God is the enemy of the aggressor."

On the 23rd of June the Grand Army crossed the Niemen in three great streams. As Napoleon rode along, his horse stumbled. "What bad luck!" cried some one. "A Roman would have turned back."

But Napoleon went on, his troops cheering as they reached the other side.

It was a barren, empty country into which they had come. No enemy even awaited them. A few horsemen watched as they marched. "Why do you come into Russia?" they asked.

"To conquer you," was the reply, and the horsemen galloped silently away, and disappeared into the forests beyond.

The weather had been very hot. Now a thunderstorm came on, and, soaked with sudden dashes of rain, the men trudged over miles of muddy road to Vilna.

It was an immense country into which Napoleon now marched; for more than half of Europe is Russia. And all this great tract of land is for the most part a plain. The only mountains are the Urals on the eastern and the Caucasus on the southern borders. There is indeed a little group, called the Valdai Hills, south of St. Petersburg, but they are not a thousand feet high. They form, however, low though they are, the main watershed of Russia.

The immense rolling plains of Russia stretch right northward to the Polar regions, and from there icy winds sweep down, unchecked by any mountain range, making winter very cold. The climate is very dry, too, and the summer hot; for, being on all sides far from the great seas, the winds have lost most of their moisture before they reach Russia.

Vilna is full of narrow, dirty streets, flanked by great houses. Here the roads to Königsberg, Warsaw, St. Petersburg, and Moscow meet and cross. And now it is a great railway junction and the centre of the timber and grain trade of Western Russia. For more than a third of Russia is covered with forests which supply timber, tar, and turpentine in great quantities. And upon the rolling plains much grain and flax and hemp are grown, although, as in Spain, the Russian peasants' ways of farming are very old-fashioned. The Russian peasant, too, is very ignorant, and lives in great misery and poverty.

CHAPTER XLVI

THE TAKING OF SMOLENSK

When Napoleon reached Vilna he found it empty. Two days before, a great part of the Russian army, which had been quartered there, had marched away. But before they went they had burned the stores and magazines. All round, the country was wasted, villages were burned, and food of every kind, both for man and horse, destroyed. This was done so that the French might find as little as possible in the way of shelter or food.

With the French army came an enormous baggage-train. But Napoleon had so long accustomed his armies to believe that they would find all they required in the countries they invaded, that this part of the army was very badly managed. Already the soldiers began to suffer from hunger.

At Vilna, Napoleon remained three weeks. Then he marched on again to Polotsk, and then to Vitepsk, on the Western Dwina. There are two rivers of that name in Russia—the one, a good navigable river, falls into the Baltic at the town of Riga; the other, the Northern Dwina, falls into the White Sea at the town of Archangel. But although it too is navigable a good way up, it has dangerous bars of sand at its mouth which prevent its being of much use. Besides, being so far north, the port of Archangel is frozen for a great part of each year. Indeed this is so with all the ports and all the rivers of Russia. But some are closed for longer some for shorter time.

All the rivers of Russia are long, and, as you would guess from the flatness of the country, they flow slowly, and they are apt to overflow their banks. Much of the country through which they pass is marshy. But one curious thing about Russian rivers is that it is nearly always the left bank which overflows. The right bank is higher, and therefore nearly all the large towns are to be found on that bank.

The right bank of a river is that on your right hand when you stand facing its mouth.

As Russia is such a large country, and as it has so little sea-coast in comparison to its size, it is a good thing that it has long rivers, and that they are navigable for such long distances inland. The Volga, which is the longest river in Europe, is connected by canals and other rivers with the Black Sea, the White Sea, and with the Baltic, so that Russia has a splendid system of inland communication.

As Napoleon advanced into the country, the Russians, who were divided into two armies, retreated. At Vitepsk there was three days of fighting. Napoleon called it three victories, but the Russians were not routed, and still retired in good order.

At last Smolensk, on the Dnieper, "the key to the gate of Russia," was reached.

Here the two Russian armies, which had been marching by different routes, joined. The part which had come from Vilna was under Barclay de Tolly. He was a cool and cautious German. But his forefathers had been Scots who had fled from Scotland at the time of the Jacobite rebellion in 1715. The other part was under Bagration, a brave and eager Russian. These two generals unfortunately hated each other. And indeed the whole army disliked Barclay, because he was a foreigner, and because he had retired instead of facing the enemy and fighting. Now, at Smolensk, the Russians made a stand. They called this town "Smolensk the Holy," because it guarded the way to their sacred city Moscow. And it was said that great misfortune would overtake Russia were Smolensk allowed to fall into the hands of the enemy.

Around and in the town a terrible fight took place. All the

autumn day cannon roared, shells screamed and burst, and a spattering hail of grapeshot thinned the ranks. When night came the Russians quietly withdrew and marched on the way to Moscow. Behind them they left their holy city a blazing ruin. The houses were mostly of wood, and from street to street the flames leaped, roaring and crackling. Clouds of sparks, columns of smoke, flew upward, glowing in the darkness. And when at dawn the French entered the city, it was to find silent streets, strewn with ashes and heaped with dead, but hardly a living man.

Napoleon had indeed taken Smolensk. But when he got it, it was only a pile of ruins, and had cost him twelve thousand men. When, however, the Russians heard that their city was lost, they were so angry that the command was taken from Barclay de Tolly and given to Kutusoff, an old general of no great skill, who had been defeated at Austerlitz. But he was a Russian, which Barclay was not.

Now, along dusty, sandy roads, past burned and deserted villages and towns, through dreary, silent, barren plains, the retreat and chase went on. The air was hot and close, the sun shone pitilessly. The men marched wearily, for they were parched with thirst and always hungry. For a month they had little to eat, except what they could find by scouring the country far and wide. At last they reached the little village of Borodino, and there found Kutusoff encamped, barring the way to Moscow.

CHAPTER XLVII

THE BURNING OF MOSCOW

For two days the armies lay opposite each other, each preparing for battle. The weather had now grown colder, and a bitter wind swept the plain, but on the 7th September the sun rose clear and bright. "It is the sun of Austerlitz," said Napoleon, as he watched it, meaning that he would have good luck that day.

Soon the thunder of battle began. Both sides fought fiercely. Forts were taken, and lost, and taken again. The battle swayed this way and that. But when at last it was over, the Russians were marching from the field, yet not in rout, but slowly and in good order. The French claimed the day, but among the eighty thousand dead, there were nearly as many of the French as of the Russian army.

Borodino is the deadliest battle of all Napoleon's wars, and it is known as "the generals' battle," for twenty-two Russian and eighteen French generals were among the slain.

Once more the chase began, the French following the Russians through country which they purposely left desolate behind them. At last, one beautiful autumn morning about a week after the battle of Borodino, Napoleon and his army caught the first sight of Moscow, from the summit of a little hill called the Hill of Salvation, which overlooks it.

"Moscow! Moscow!" The cry ran down the lines. To the weary men Moscow was the haven of rest towards which they had been struggling those hundreds and hundreds of dreary miles. Now it lay before them, glittering white in the sunshine, with its many-coloured roofs, gilded domes, spires, and turrets. "The Asiatic town of countless churches, Moscow the Holy," cried Napoleon, reining in his horse. "There at last is the famous town. It was time!"

Until Peter the Great built St. Petersburg, Moscow was the capital of Russia, and lying as it does in the heart of the country, far away from other European lands, it is there that one sees the true Russian national life.

Moscow has grown up round its fort, called the Kremlin, which stands upon a slight hill, and seems to dominate the city. "Over Moscow there is only the Kremlin; over the Kremlin there is only the heavens." Within the battlemented wall of this fortress are gathered churches and palaces, and round them cling all the memories and history of the people. To the Russian it is holy ground.

Moscow is also the seat of the oldest Russian university, and it is the busiest and most commercial inland town, being the centre of the Russian railways. It is upon a navigable river, and has splendid communication in all directions by the Volga, Oka, Don, Dnieper, and Western Dwina. It lies near one of the chief Russian coalfields. It has cotton and silk factories, and is altogether a place of wealth and importance, and its broad streets are full of a busy, stirring life.

But when Napoleon and his army marched through the streets, they were silent and deserted. Here and there a timid or scowling face might be seen. But the streets echoed with a hollow sound, and the empty houses stared down upon the soldiers with closed shutters, like sightless eyes.

For days every one who could leave the city had been hurrying away, and the roads had been full of a constant stream of clattering carriages and rumbling carts laden with people and their goods. The night before Napoleon had entered, the troops too had gone. All night long the steady tramp, tramp, had sounded through the streets. The great military stores had been burned or destroyed, the prisons opened, and the prisoners set free, the fire-engines made useless, and the great city, mostly built of wood, left to the mercy of the rabble and the foe.

Scarcely two hours after the last soldier had gone, the French arrived. And when they found the city silent and empty, they broke into the deserted houses, robbing and wrecking them, decking themselves in ridiculous finery, drinking wildly, until the army became a drunken mob.

But at last the noise of laughter and carouse ceased, and the city sank to rest. The weary soldiers, who for many weeks had slept under the open sky and on the bare ground, slept this night in splendid palaces and on soft couches, wrapped in silken covers.

But in the middle of the night the cry of fire arose. Soon the city was bright with flames, and morning dawned before they were put out.

Again, when night came, the fire broke out, and not in one place only, but in many. From every quarter, north, south, east, and west, fire burst, until the city was a blazing sea of flame. A strong wind arose, blowing the flames, now here, now there, till palaces and churches, shops and houses, were wrapped in fire, and sank together in piles of charred and blackened ashes.

For two days Napoleon gloomily watched the fearful destruction from the Kremlin. Then that too took fire, and at last, yielding to the entreaties of his officers, Napoleon rode from the burning town, through a whirlwind of flame, a raging hail of sparks, and rolling clouds of smoke.

He took refuge in a palace belonging to the Czar which was beyond the city. But even there the heat of the flames was so great that the stones were hot to touch. Whenever the fire seemed to die down in one place, it kindled again in another. But at last, when four-fifths of the city lay in blackened ruin, when there was little left to burn, the flames ceased.

Napoleon then returned to the Kremlin, and there he awaited an answer to a letter which he had written to the Czar by the light of the burning city. It was a letter proposing terms of peace. But no answer to it ever came.

CHAPTER XLVIII

THE RETREAT FROM MOSCOW

Day after day passed. At first there had been food enough for the great army—splendid wines and dainty fare, such as they were little accustomed to, but they soon gave out. Now of bread there was none, and only horseflesh for meat. The Russians had swept the country bare. It was in vain that the French soldiers scoured it in search of food. It was in vain that Napoleon issued proclamations to the peasants, telling them that they would be well paid for anything that they might bring. Their hatred of the French was such that not all the gold in the country could tempt them to Moscow. They would rather have cut off their right hands than have helped Napoleon in the slightest.

The autumn had been unusually warm, the sunny weather had lasted late, but at length it came to an end. A slight snow fell as a warning that the fearful Russian winter was about to begin. It is a winter of keen cold, such as the French had no knowledge of. They were ill fed and worse clothed, and in no way fit to endure it.

Again Napoleon wrote to Alexander. Again no answer was returned.

Then, seeing the uselessness and danger of trying to spend the winter in a barren country, hundreds and hundreds of miles from his own kingdom, Napoleon gave the order to march back.

Napoleon had to face defeat. Yet even to himself he would not own it.

"Moscow has been found not to be a good military post," he writes. "It is necessary for the army to breathe in a wider space."

At first Napoleon tried to march southward, so as not to return over the desolate country of his former track. But he was soon turned back by a Russian force, and obliged to march the way that he had come.

The sick and wounded were left behind, so as not to burden the army. But every soldier was laden with booty. Gold and silver plate, silk and gems were piled in wheelbarrows, beautiful carriages were laden with all kinds of spoil, and a train of Russian prisoners marched bowed beneath heavy loads.

So the march began. But soon the road was strewn with these splendid spoils. Hunger, fearful, gnawing hunger, took hold upon the men. There was nothing to eat but horseflesh. When a horse died, the men fell upon it like hungry wolves, tearing it to pieces. They were ready to kill each other for a few potatoes or a handful of rye. All order, all discipline was lost. Many broke from the ranks, and wandering about, seeking vainly for food, perished on the barren steppes.

Harassed by Cossacks, the wretched army still pressed forward. Then came the snow, and with it bitter cold. The snow fell and fell, blotting out the road, blotting out every landmark. Blinded by the whirling flakes, chilled to the bone by cutting winds, the men wandered on, hardly knowing whither. Numbed and frozen, unable to crawl farther, many fell, and the white snow became their winding-sheet. At night perhaps they bivouacked, and in the morning a circle of white mounds alone told where they had lain down to sleep their last sleep.

Pursuing Russians killed those who straggled behind. Often they had no strength to resist. Sometimes even they had no arms, for their muskets would drop from their frozen fingers and be left in the snow.

Yet, through all the misery and cold and famine, a few lived and struggled on. "Smolensk! Smolensk!" they said. That was their goal, the paradise of rest and plenty to which they pressed.

But when Smolensk was at last reached, they found neither rest nor plenty there. The town was as much a ruin as Moscow had been. The stores of food and clothes were exhausted.

After a few days' halt the retreat continued. Near the town of Borisoff the river Beresina had to be crossed by two frail bridges. And here one of the most terrible scenes of the war took place.

While the French crossed they were attacked by the Russians. As men frantic with terror crushed on to the bridges, one of them gave way, and all upon it were thrown into the half-frozen river below. Over the second bridge the French now rushed madly, trampling and killing each other in their haste, shot down in crowds by the Russian bullets. Shrieks of terror and pain filled the air, mingling with the crash and thunder of the Russian guns and the savage cheers of the Russian soldiers. Twelve thousand at least perished at this fearful crossing. The rest continued their march of agony towards Vilna.

Ten days later a miserable, ragged, limping crowd crept into that town. "Remove all strangers from Vilna," Napoleon had written. "The army is not beautiful to look upon just now." But ere the ragged remnant of the once Grand Army had reached Vilna, Napoleon had deserted it. He had heard that there was a rising in Paris. So leaving his soldiers to their misery, wrapped in furs, he hurried as fast as horses could carry him homeward, by Warsaw, Dresden, Erfurt, and Mainz, to Paris.

Meanwhile the miserable spectre of an army staggered on, chased by the pitiless Cossacks. At last, in the middle of December, they crossed the Niemen, and found a refuge for a time in and near Königsberg. Of all the magnificent army that had set out to conquer Russia, not twenty thousand famine-stricken men returned.

The Retreat from Moscow

CHAPTER XLIX

NAPOLEON'S LAST GREAT VICTORY

It should not be forgotten that of all the Grand Army scarcely a sixth were French, and of those the best officers and men returned. So almost at once Napoleon was able to raise a new army. True, most of the new recruits were boys under twenty, but the magic of his name was still so great that they were eager to fight for him. And he had need of all this eagerness, for Prussia, following the example of Spain, and encouraged by the news of Napoleon's awful defeat in Russia, resolved to fight once more for freedom.

Men rich and poor, old and young, flocked to the standard. Ladies brought their jewels, and the Czar of Russia marched to meet his old friend, whom, it is true, he had forsaken, and almost betrayed, at Tilsit. It was at Breslau that they met. Tears came into the eyes of the old King as he greeted Alexander. "Wipe them," said he; "they are the last tears that Napoleon will ever cause you to shed."

The Prussian leader was Blücher, a rough old man, but brave and loving his country well, and loved by his men. It was he who, after Jena, held out longest against Napoleon, only surrendering when resistance was useless and hopeless.

By the middle of April Napoleon was upon the banks of the Saale. He crossed the river, and it was at the village of Grosz-Gor-schen that the first battle of the new war was fought. It was fierce and long, and after it was over the Prussian and Russian allies fell back to Leipsig. But to Napoleon it was no victory. He took no prisoners, and nearly as many French as allies lay dead upon the field.

Leipsig, where the allies now lay, is a garrison town and head-quarters of part of the German army. It is also one of the important commercial towns of Germany, and is the centre of the German book trade. There is here a very interesting Museum of the Book Trade, which shows how books have been made in all ages.

The trade in books at Leipsig brought trade in leather for binding, and its nearness to the Saxony coalfields, and its position at the point where many roads join, have all helped to make the town a trade centre. It is one of the largest fur markets in the world, besides having trade in cloth, linen, glass, and many other things.

From Leipsig the allies fell back to Dresden, and from Dresden they still fell back to Bautzen, a busy little town upon the Spree. Here, upon the wooded hills above the Spree, they took their stand, and here another battle was fought.

For two days this battle lasted—two beautiful spring days—and again the bloodshed was terrible. Again the allies drew back, but they went calmly and coolly; there was no flight, no disorder; they lost neither guns nor men. "What," cried Napoleon, "all that bloodshed, and no results! Not a gun, not a prisoner! These people will not leave me a nail."

At last, after these two uncertain victories, if victories they could be called, Napoleon agreed to a truce, which was signed on 4th June 1813. Both sides wanted time to make new plans, and to get their armies into better order. A Peace Congress now began at Prague, the capital of Bohemia, which is a country of hills and valleys. Prague is full of old houses and monuments, and its university is the oldest of German-speaking universities. It is a city of the past, but a city of the present too. It is near a field of iron ore, and also near the chief coalfield of Bohemia, and has manufactures of machinery and other things.

But the Peace Congress which now sat here was of little use for Napoleon was not willing to give up the smallest part of his conquests. And after nine weeks' truce, war broke out again, with this difference, that Austria had joined the allies, and Napoleon had another foe to fight.

Napoleon had spent the time of the truce drilling and perfecting his army. Now his forces lay at Buntzlau in Silesia; at Zittau, a linen manufacturing town on the borders of Bohemia; at Pirna, which guards the chief pass from Bohemia; at Leipsig; and at Dresden.

If you look on the map you will see that the army thus formed a circle round Dresden. And at Dresden, in the centre of the circle, was Napoleon. In a larger circle, facing the French, lay the armies of the allies, at Prague, at Berlin, and at Breslau. Upon this mighty chess-board the men now moved.

At first the allies were successful. Twice the French were defeated. Then the fight closed round Dresden. Here there was a two days' battle, fought in dashing rain, on fields of mud. Such torrents of rain poured upon the men that both they and their weapons were soaked. Guns became useless. It was a hand-to-hand fight with sword and bayonet. It ended in victory to the French. It was Napoleon's last great victory.

CHAPTER L

A LAST GOOD-BYE

While Napoleon had been winning the battle of Dresden, Blücher had defeated the French not far from Liegnitz, on the Katzbach, a tributary of the Oder. It was at this battle that Blucher got the name "Marshal Forwards" by which his men loved to call him. He waited steadily until a good many Frenchmen had crossed the river, then he said "Now I have enough Frenchmen on this side. Now Forwards!" The battle was won and Blücher earned a new name.

Three days after Katzbach, when the French were pursuing the allies, who were falling back from Dresden to Prague, they were cut to pieces at Kulm, in Bohemia. A week later Marshal Ney was defeated at Dennewitz, near the little town of Juterbog. Thus in a fortnight Napoleon had gained one battle and his generals had lost five.

The days when by one victory he could conquer a kingdom were over. "The chess-board is very confused," said Napoleon.

For the rest of the month the Emperor moved restlessly about, now into Bohemia, now into Silesia, at length to Leipsig. And it was round that town that the last battle of the campaign was fought—the Battle of the Nations it has been called.

On the 16th of October the battle began. On the 19th Napoleon and his beaten army were streaming across the Elbe, leaving behind them thousands dead, thousands more prisoners, besides hundreds of cannon, stores, and ammunition, and, greatest of all, a mighty empire shattered and crumbling into dust. It was just a year since the Grand Army had begun its fearful march from Moscow.

Without an army Napoleon could not hold his vast conquests. Without an army he could only be King of the French, and of all his great forces only about forty thousand men hurried towards the borders of France.

Napoleon marched by Erfurt, where a few years before he had been surrounded by such splendour. At Hanau, a quaint little town famous for its gold and silver work and diamond-cutting, the Austrians barred the path. But Napoleon cut his way through, and reached Frankfurt-on-Main, one of the important commercial cities of Germany, sheltered by sunny vine-clad hills, and the centre of many railroads leading out to all parts. At last at Mainz, where the Rhine and the Main join, Napoleon crossed the Rhine, and was once more in his own land.

And when the pursuing Germans reached the Rhine, and saw it wind glittering and beautiful before them, between its vine-clad hills, they raised a cry of joy, "The Rhine! the Rhine!" And falling upon their knees, they thanked God that the invaders had been driven beyond the river, and that at last their country was their own again.

Although the Rhine rises in Switzerland, and reaches the sea through Holland, it is the greatest of German rivers. "Father Rhine," the Germans call it. It is navigable almost from the borders of Switzerland to its mouth, but it is most important below Mannheim. By means of canals it is connected with many other rivers—the Rhône, Saône, Scheldt, Meuse, and Danube. It serves as a great highway of commerce, helping, among other things, to spread abroad the coal and iron of which, next to Great Britain, Germany produces the most in Europe.

The beauty of the Rhine, its vine-clad hills topped with grey old castles in every stage of ruin, brings many visitors every year, These vine-clad hills produce, too, many famous white wines. Sheltered by the Vosges on one side and by the Schwartzwald on the other, the Rhine valley from Basel to Mainz is warmer and drier than many parts of Germany. But perhaps the best wine-growing districts are from Mainz to Bonn.

All over Europe the nations now began to throw off French yoke. The Dutch and Germans tore the tricolour down, and once more their own standards floated out on the breeze. Everywhere the German fortresses which were held by French soldiers surrendered or were taken.

On the 9th of November Napoleon reached Paris, and here the allies sent to him conditions of peace. Much that he had conquered was to be given back, but not all. The Rhine was still to be the boundary of France. Belgium, Savoy, and Nice also were left to him. But Napoleon did not yet believe in his defeat. He would not give up any of his conquests. So the allies marched into France, and another war began.

The allies fought, not with France, they said, but with Napoleon. "We thought to find peace before we touched your borders; now we come to find it here."

Many of the people of France had been weary of Napoleon and his wars. But now that the foe had marched into their beloved land, they rose to defend it. Napoleon once more prepared to take the field.

On Sunday, 23rd January, he held a last and splendid reception in the palace of the Tuileries. When the courtiers were gathered, Napoleon walked into the hall with the Empress Marie Louise and his little son, now just three years old. Holding one by either hand, he turned to his court. "Gentlemen," he said, "France is invaded. I go to put myself at the head of the army. I leave to you that which I hold dearest—my wife and son."

Two days later Napoleon said good-bye to Marie Louise. They never saw each other again, for when Napoleon returned to Paris his power was broken, and Marie Louise refused to share the fortunes of a fallen King.

CHAPTER LI

THE EMPEROR OF ELBA

At Brienne, where Napoleon had fought with snowballs in his boyish days, he now fought with more deadly weapons. At first he was successful, then he lost. Then in four days, with his old quickness, he won four victories, at Champaubert, Montmirail, Chateau-Thierry, and Vauchamps.

Never perhaps in all his triumphant campaigns had Napoleon shown more his great genius as a soldier. Nearly always he had fought against armies smaller in numbers or less well drilled than his own. Now he had to fight against far greater numbers, and his soldiers were for the most part young and untrained—"Marie Louises" they were called, from the name of the Empress. Yet still Napoleon wrung victories and triumphs from the foe.

But at last, after the war had been flung this way and that, after marches and counter-marches, after taking of towns and burning of villages, until Marne, Aube, and Aisne, some of the fairest provinces of France, had become a desert, the allies began to march on Paris.

Round that fair city, which never since the days of the Maid of Orleans had heard the shouts of a foreign foe, the horrors of war raged. For one long day Prussians filled with bitter hate against their conqueror, half-savage Russians, Austrians, Dutch, people of every country which Napoleon had enslaved, surged in a red circle of fire and death about the city. Then it yielded.

On the 31st of March 1814 the Emperor of Russia and the King of Prussia rode side by side into the city, and passed through the streets filled with people, some sullen and angry, others rejoicing as at a great deliverance, and shouting, "Long live the Emperor Alexander Long live the King of Prussia!'

Marie Louise had already fled, taking her little son with her. Napoleon, hurrying from the battlefields of Champagne, reached Fontainebleau, to hear that the fight was over.

"On to Paris!" he cried.

"Sire, it is too late," replied an officer. "Paris has yielded."

Napoleon had been Emperor of half Europe. He had been a king of kings, making and unmaking them at will. In a few years he had built up his mighty empire. In a few months he had lost it bit by bit, until now not even his own capital remained to him. There the allies ruled, and on the 2nd April 1814 the Senate declared that Napoleon had ceased to reign.

But still Napoleon did not believe that all was lost. At Fontainebleau he reviewed his troops. His Old Guard, men who had been with him through every campaign, were still eager to fight for him. "To Paris! to Paris!" they shouted.

But the officers were weary of it all. "We have had enough of war," said one. "Let us not begin a civil war."

So at length, seeing no help for it, Napoleon wrote out and signed his abdication—that is, the paper by which he gave up all claim to the crown of France. "The allied Powers having declared that the Emperor Napoleon is the only cause which prevents peace being brought back to Europe, he, faithful to his oaths, is ready to descend from the throne, to leave France, and even give up his life for the good of his country."

With his own hand Napoleon had placed the crown upon his head; with his own hand he now signed away his power. A few days later the Peninsular War came to an end with the battle of Toulouse, in which the French were defeated. Had the armies in Spain only known what was happening in Paris, there would have been no need to fight that battle at all.

On the 20th of April Napoleon said good-bye to his troops in the courtyard of Fontainebleau. His men loved and admired him still. Tears rolled down their bronzed cheeks, sobs choked them.

"I cannot embrace you all," he cried, "but I embrace you in your general." And putting his arms round him, he kissed him. He kissed the standard too, the splendid eagle of France, which had led them so often under burning suns or cloudy skies, through the parching heat of summer or the snows of winter.

Then the fallen Emperor stepped into his carriage and was whirled away southwards. He was an Emperor still, for the allies allowed him to keep his title. But his empire was only the little island of Elba.

At first, as Napoleon drove through France, the people cheered him on his way. But as he went farther and farther south, where the people had never loved him, and where they now hated him, he was greeted with curses fierce and loud. The peasants cared little for "glory." They only knew that their sons and brothers and fathers had been taken from them, never to return. They knew that the vineyards were untilled and the fields a barren waste, for the workers lay dead in many a distant land. So they cursed the man whose pride had brought such sorrow and poverty upon them.

At last the anger and hatred of the people grew so great that Napoleon was forced to disguise himself as an Austrian officer to save himself from their fury. And thus he fled southwards until he reached the shore, and there set sail for Elba.

CHAPTER LII

CORPORAL VIOLET

Although the peasants of France had cursed Napoleon as he passed, the people of Elba welcomed him gladly. And here for a little time the great Emperor played at empire. His empire was not more than ninety square miles in extent. Like Corsica, Elba is full of hills, and has a rough, jagged coastline. The soil is fertile enough, but is not greatly cultivated, and the chief industry is mining. The iron mines of Elba are famous, and the ore is so good that it is much used for making Bessemer steel. Bessemer was a man who found out, and gave his name to, a way of changing iron into steel.

Elba has no coal, so most of the iron is exported to France, Britain, and the United States. There are also marble and alabaster quarries, tin, lead, and silver mines; but the iron mines are the most important.

Here Napoleon had his little army of a few hundred men. Here he held court with as great state and ceremony as in the Tuileries, although his palace was little more than an ordinary country-house.

Meanwhile the brother of Louis XVI., whom the French had beheaded, was proclaimed King of France. He called himself Louis XVIII., as the little son of Louis XVI. had been called Louis XVII., although he never reigned, but died in prison in 1795, while France was still a republic and Napoleon a struggling soldier.

Louis was old, fat, and feeble. He was fond of eating and drinking, and the people called him, not Louis Dix-huit (18th), but Louis des huîtres (of the oysters). He was not stupid, but he was not clever enough to rule at such a time, when all France, and indeed all Europe, was turned upside down, and full of discontent, every one struggling for something, they hardly knew what.

When the French soldiers who had been imprisoned in German fortresses were set free and came back to France, the discontent grew worse. For they, having spent so many years fighting, could not settle down to a life of peace. They longed for their great leader again, and he was soon weary of playing at empire in his little island.

It began to be whispered that the great Emperor was not gone for always. "He will come again with the spring flowers," said his friends. So the violet came to be his emblem. His friends wore violets. Pictures of bunches of violets were sold, in which, if you look carefully enough, you can see among the flowers the faces of Napoleon, of Marie Louise, and of the little King of Rome. "Do you like violets?" people asked each other. If the answer was "Yes," then it was known that person was not a friend; but if the answer was "Ah, well," the person was a friend. So there was much mysterious talk of "Corporal Violet." But all this plotting was very open, and no one paid much attention to it, and nothing would have come of it had Napoleon himself not been weary of his island.

He had been there just eleven months when he made up his mind once more to try his fortune. He escaped from Elba easily enough, and landed near Cannes on March 1st, 1815.

Cannes is on the south coast of France, and was easily reached from Elba. It has a mild and dry climate, and, like the places on the Riviera, has become a favourite spot for invalids to pass the winter.

From Cannes Napoleon marched to Grasse, famous for its acres of flowers, especially roses, which are grown for scent-making.

Anxiously Napoleon hurried on to Grenoble. This town, lying upon the spurs of the Alps, guarding the routes from the Mont Cenis and the Little St. Bernard, is a very strong position. It is the centre of the French glove trade, and for forty miles around all the villages are engaged in the manufacture. Skins are supplied from the flocks of kids which feed upon the hill slopes around, and many are imported also.

And here it was that an army was sent to stop Napoleon. He already had a little army, for he had brought his soldiers with him from Elba; but few others had joined. Now he advanced against the enemy alone. "Soldiers," he cried, "if there is one amongst you who desires to kill his Emperor, he can do so. Here I am." And he threw back his coat as if awaiting the blow. But not a weapon was raised. Instead, a shout of "Long live the Emperor!" rang out, and every man marched over to his old leader's side.

At Lyons the Bourbon generals fled, and Napoleon entered the city in triumph. Ney, one of Napoleon's old generals, whom he had called "the bravest of the brave," marched to stop him, vowing to bring his old master back in an iron cage, like a wild beast. But he had not marched far before he too declared for Napoleon, and at Auxerre joined his army.

And so, as on and on Napoleon passed, the little man in the big grey coat, which the soldiers knew and loved, drew them to himself. His army grew larger and larger. Men tore the white cockade of the Bourbons from their hats, and trampled it under foot. Once more the tricolour was everywhere.

In the middle of the night King Louis fled from Paris towards Belgium, and at last, on 19th March, Napoleon once more reached Fontainebleau. The next day he entered Paris.

While the allies were gathered at Vienna trying to bring order into disordered Europe, they had been suddenly startled by the news that Napoleon had left Elba, and was making his way to Paris. They had not agreed very well, but now this new danger made them forget their quarrels. Quickly they gathered their soldiers, and by June armies were marching against France from all sides. From Russia, Prussia, Sardinia, Austria, from Holland and Belgium and the German states, and, not least, from Britain, came troops.

But Napoleon did not wait for France to be invaded. He

marched northward. He hoped with his usual quick daring to win some splendid battle, and with one stroke shatter the power of the allies, and seat himself again upon the throne of France.

CHAPTER LIII

NAPOLEON'S LAST BATTLE

It was in Belgium that Napoleon's last great battle was fought. The Duke of Wellington commanded a great part of the allied troops which were gathered there. Some of these occupied Enghien, Brain le Comte, and Nivelles; others lay at Brussels and Ghent. His cavalry was at Halle, Oudenarde, and Gramont.

The Prussian troops, led by grim old Blücher, lay along the banks of the Meuse and the Sambre, occupying Liège, Givet, Namur, and Charleroi. Brussels is the capital of Belgium. But at Ghent there was King Louis, and whether Napoleon would march on Brussels or on Ghent, or by which route he would come, the allies did not know.

But at last, on 15th June, Napoleon attacked the Prussians at Charleroi. They fell back to Ligny, and there the next day a stern battle was fought between the French and the Prussians. In the heat and dust of a summer's day, from two o'clock until the sun went down in the darkness and rain of a sudden thunderstorm, the battle raged. Napoleon won the victory, but lost many men; and the Prussians and their leader were as defiant as ever.

At the same time Ney attacked the British, who were now gathered round the farmhouse of Quatre Bras (fours arms), so called because it stands where four roads meet from Charleroi, Brussels, Nivelles, and Namur. Here too the fighting was fierce and terrible, but the French were driven back. Napoleon, however, had done what he had meant to do. He had separated the two armies, and he hoped to be able to beat that under Wellington before Blücher could come to help him. But Blücher and Wellington had promised to try to keep together and help each other.

It was upon the 18th of June, upon the field of Waterloo, that Napoleon made his last stand, fought his last fight—and lost.

The night had been wet and blustry. In the morning rain still fell, and the fair fields of Waterloo about the farms of La Haye Sainte and Hougoment were sodden and marshy, and it was not until nearly twelve that the battle began. All day long, under a cloudy, stormy sky, the battle raged. It was a fight of all the nations, and in Wellington's army alone five languages were spoken.

And while at Waterloo the thunder of war roared and crashed, Blücher with his Prussians was toiling over rain-soaked roads, his cannon sinking axle-deep in mud, his men splashing and ploughing through deep pools, stumbling wearily onward to join the battle. "We can go no farther," they cried despairingly.

"We must, my children; I have given my word to Wellington. You would not have me break it," replied Blücher. So they struggled on, but it was late in the afternoon before they reached the battlefield.

The end of the long struggle was now near. Napoleon ordered his Old Guard, which he had kept in reserve, to advance. But when he saw them bend and then break and scatter before the British charge, he turned deadly pale. "Why, they are in confusion!" he cried, hardly able to believe it possible. "All is lost. Let us save ourselves."

In utter rout and panic the French fled from the field. The wearied British soldiers left the pursuit to the Prussians. Under the light of the moon and till the dawning of the day the chase went on. For many miles the roads were ghastly and horrible. Again and again the French tried to take refuge in the villages by the way. Again and again they were driven forth, fleeing before the terrible hurrah of the exultant Prussians, who slaughtered them without mercy.

To Charleroi, to Philippeville, and on to Paris fled Napoleon,

Waterloo

tears of anger and despair running down his pale cheeks. On the night of the 20th of June he reached Paris.

On the 19th the capital had been rejoicing over the victory of Ligny. On the 21st came the fearful news that the Emperor had returned alone, and that the great army of France was no more.

And now Napoleon learned that, as he was no longer great and successful, the people of Paris did not want him. Of the soldiers who adored him few were left. So once more he abdicated. His second reign, which had lasted only a hundred days, was over.

By his own people Napoleon was ordered to leave Paris. By his own people he was hurried southward to Rochefort, the great arsenal and naval port of southern France.

He was ordered to leave France, but British men-of-war were watching every port, and escape was impossible. So at last he gave himself up to the commander of the *Bellerophon*, and was taken to England. To the Prince Regent he wrote "I come to seat myself on the hearth of the British people. I put myself under the protection of their laws, which I claim from your Royal Highness as the most powerful, the most constant, and the most generous of my enemies."

Sadly Napoleon watched the shores of France disappear. He never set foot in France again, never more saw its sunny shores. He was only forty-five, but his life of splendour and excitement was done.

It had been Napoleon's dream to conquer Britain, and add these islands to his empire. Now as a fugitive he was not even allowed to land there. He was kept on the *Bellerophon* until a letter was brought to him which told him that "General Bonaparte" was to be sent to St. Helena, a little island in the South Atlantic.

CHAPTER LIV

THE END

And now the great Emperor who had ruled over millions of people was once more only General Bonaparte. Perhaps it would have been better had the British left him his title. But they had never acknowledged him as Emperor, and it seemed too late to begin now. It would have been only an empty title, for now at St. Helena Napoleon was not free, as he had been at Elba.

At Elba, small though his empire was, Napoleon was still a ruler. He could still make laws and levy taxes, was still surrounded by an army and a court. At St. Helena he was a prisoner, and a prisoner in a lonely island 2000 leagues from Europe, 900 leagues from the nearest continent.

St. Helena is very small, not more than twenty-one miles all round, and from a distance it looks like a shapeless mass of black rock rising out of the sea, and topped by a cone. This is Diana Peak, the highest point in the island. It is part of an old volcano, and the soil is chiefly lava, but, especially upon the western side, the island is fertile, and side by side plants of both tropical and temperate climates grow. Here may be found apples and tea, breadfruit, plums, nutmegs, and gooseberries, all within the space of a few miles. Many of the slopes, too, are a blaze of yellow broom in springtime.

At James Town, where Napoleon landed, there is a safe harbour, protected by natural rocks of lava. It is a British coaling-station, and is still kept fortified. But to Napoleon it seemed a hateful place. And little wonder. After his life of splendour and excitement, it was terrible to be shut away in this lonely island in the middle of the wide ocean. Yet it was only in such a lonely place that Napoleon could be allowed any freedom at all. In Europe he would have been shut up in some fortress, or, if Blücher had had his way, he would have been put to death.

At St. Helena he had a comfortable house, £12,000 a year to spend, he had his own servants and officers about him, and twelve miles of country through which he might wander at will, without being watched. Yet he was miserable. It was little wonder. He who had played with kings and kingdoms, making and unmaking them, moving them here and there at will, like chessmen on a board, had now nothing to do.

He who had been dreaded by half the world was now of no importance. It mattered not whether he lived or died. So the dreary years dragged on in petty quarrels about petty things, in reading, writing, and chess-playing.

Then after five years the great conqueror lay dying. As he lay, already muttering and unconscious, a great storm swept the island. It dashed the waves against the rocky shore; it bent, broke, and uprooted the willows about his house. But Napoleon lay unheeding it; his wandering mind was dreaming of other days. "France-army-Josephine," he muttered. Then he lay still. The wind too sank to rest, and when the golden sun of May, shining once more over calm blue waters, slid beneath the waves, the restless, stormy spirit passed with it.

A few days later, followed reverently by those few of his friends who had clung to him to the last, sharing his lonely exile, he was laid to rest, under the willow trees where he had often sat. British soldiers carried the coffin, upon which was laid the sword and cloak he had worn at Marengo, British soldiers fired a volley and lowered their banners in salute over the grave of their great enemy. And there they left him in a nameless tomb.

Eighteen years later, in the darkness of an October midnight, by the faint light of lanterns, the coffin was once more dug up and carried away to France, with the permission of the British Government.

At the Hôtel des Invalides in Paris it was received by the nobles and the King of France, who, Bourbon though he was, desired to do honour to the great Emperor dead. "Sire, I present the body of the Emperor Napoleon," said the Prince de Joinville, who had brought it from St. Helena. "I receive it in the name of France," replied the King.

So for the last time the greatest soldier the world has ever seen was laid to rest beside the Seine, among his people, as he himself had wished.

THE END